Racing

to

Pittsburgh

by

Donald Hricik

Strategic Book Group

Strategic Book Group
P.O. Box 333
Durham CT 06422
www.StrategicBookClub.com

ISBN: 978-1-60976-122-6

Printed in the United States of America

Book Design: Bonita S. Watson

To Lynne, Brian, Kevin, Lauren, and Michael

Contents

Part II

Acknowledgements

The faculty and staff of University Hospitals Case Medical Center and the Ireland Cancer Center.

A portion of proceeds from sales of this book will be donated to the Leukemia and Lymphoma Society, in recognition of that organization's efforts to support the patients and families that deal with acute leukemia and other life-threatening malignancies.

Prologue

When a child develops acute leukemia, family members usually get closer to God. When a second member of the same family is stricken, it's time to start asking God some serious questions.

Part 1

One

Early Rounds —
September 2001

With the Labor Day weekend barely over, the morning air was cool — more like fall than summer — but the skies were clear as Dan Ulek barreled up I-271, heading for the Cleveland Medical Center. *Good flying weather — a rarity for Cleveland.* His spirits were high as he mentally prepared for another trip to Europe that afternoon. Yes, he needed a break. But on days like this, he felt that the world was his stage and that he was prepared to deliver one of his expert medical presentations at any time, anywhere on the planet.

It had been an exhausting summer and his wife, Kathy, talked to him seriously about cutting back on his work and travel schedule. She was concerned that Dan was showing signs of depression, fully aware of his family history. She was also furious that, for the third year in a row, he had agreed to cover the inpatient heart transplant ward for junior colleagues during the precious summer months. For Dan, it was a reasonable way of paying in advance for all the coverage he would need for travel during the remainder of the academic year, beginning today.

"When the twins graduate from high school in two years, for all intents and purposes, your children will be gone forever," Kathy pointed out during their bedtime conversation the night before. But quality time with the kids was something that Dan had sacrificed long ago. Until recently, it seemed that he and Kathy agreed that this was one component of the price of success. Now it had become a source of marital friction.

"Next year should be better. And by the way, I am not depressed," he said, as he had repeated innumerable times during the past few months in response to his wife's concerns. "It's just been a very busy summer."

Secretly, he worried that the stressful summer had indeed brought on *paradoxical* signs of depression — not the typical weight loss and insomnia — but overeating and excessive sleepiness, just like he observed in his bipolar father and sister over the years. Each of them was treated with lithium. Dan knew that the side effects of that drug played a role in his father's death. His sister attempted suicide on at least two occasions — once by overdosing on lithium and pain pills. He had never been convinced that pharmacologic therapy was beneficial in the treatment of depression or even manic-depression, and he certainly had no desire to go down that road.

Earlier in the week, he did agree to Kathy's demand that he have a medical checkup. "You're 52 years old. How can you take care of patients when you don't take care of yourself?"

Indeed, Dan had avoided medical care for his entire adult life and had been treating himself for not-so-mild hypertension for almost ten years. Among other things, he did not want a patient-doctor relationship with a personal friend or colleague. He finally arranged to see Tom Kingsfield, a well-respected and highly recommended young internist, at the Suburban Group Clinic. After a morning of medical history-taking, a stress test, routine blood work, and a "complete" physical (read: digital rectal examination), young Tom agreed that Dan was not depressed. "A little more exercise, maybe drop fifteen or twenty pounds, and a routine colonoscopy sometime in the next year." Dan liked Tom. *Good advice, except for the colonoscopy.* He made a mental promise to have yearly checkups going forward.

Heading for the Cedar Road off-ramp, he clicked on his cell phone, speed-dialing the transplant ward, knowing that the inpatient transplant coordinator and residents usually pre-rounded an hour before he arrived for formal attending rounds. He had just returned from a meeting in New York and was gone for only two and a half days, but the number of patients and the severity of their medical problems could change in a flash on the transplant service. He was hoping for a quiet service this morning.

"Good morning Tower 10, this is Dr. Ulek. Is Deb Hepner on the floor?" The ward receptionist put him on hold and Deb, the inpatient coordinator, picked up the phone a few moments later. "Lightning rounds, okay Deb?"

"Well if it isn't Visiting Professor Ulek. To what do we owe this pleasure? And it's only 7:00 a.m."

"Lighten up, Deb. I have a 2:30 flight to Paris through Newark, so I need to get rounds out of the way quickly. What's the body count?"

"Not too bad, only eight patients in the Tower. But Darlene May is still in the ICU and now she's on CVVH."

"Why did Renal switch her from regular dialysis to continuous dialysis?"

"She's on pressors now and systolic blood pressures are between 80 and 90. They claim they can't do regular dialysis with blood pressures that low."

"Can you call the residents and ask them to meet me in the ICU at 7:30? We'll start there and then head for the top of the Tower and work our way down."

Life would be easier if the hospital would make a simple effort to house all transplant patients on a single ward. Instead,

they often were scattered throughout as many as eight different wards. Dan figured that rounds were extended by at least an
hour a day because of the additional walking mandated by this
practice. If the designated transplant floor was full with other
general surgery patients, a transplant patient would get admitted
to a non-designated floor. According to the hospital administrators, there was too much time, effort, and money involved in
transferring the patient to the appropriate floor thereafter. It was
another example of the hospital cutting corners at the expense of
the time of their doctors. Making the problem even worse was
the fact that most attending physicians did rounds twice daily
— once to make decisions with the team of residents and nurses,
and a second time on their own, sometimes late in the day, to
write their progress notes. The written notes were necessary to
assure all of the auditing regulatory agencies that, yes, attending physicians actually *were* involved in the care of the patients.
Who needed an exercise program? A month on service was like
running five miles a day.

"No problem. I'll notify the troops and meet you in the ICU,"
said Deb. "By the way, Hurtuk just went to the OR to do another
transplant. That's three in eight days. We're on target to do fifty-
five, maybe sixty for the year."

Shit. Volume meant everything in the heart transplant business and normally he'd be happy to hear about a new transplant.
But he had just returned from speaking at a symposium in New
York on one of his off-weekends. By the time Hurtuk was finished with today's heart transplant, Dan would be well on his
way to Paris, and there wouldn't be time to touch base with Jack
or his surgical team between trips. This would just fuel Jack's
subtle allegations that Dan had become more of a world traveler
than a transplant doctor.

"Deb, does Jack know I'm coming in early to do rounds?"
he asked.

"Well, he didn't say. I think he was preoccupied with the
case — cold ischemia time was getting close to four hours and
he wanted to get the chest open. It was a really good donor

— nineteen year old male with a gunshot wound to the head — it was on the news and in the *Plain Dealer* over the weekend. But you know Hurtuk — never happy unless the cold time is under four hours."

Busting my chops to do early rounds and all I'll hear are the visiting professor jokes. He actually could have skipped rounds today and asked one of his junior colleagues to cover but, between New York and Paris, that would have amounted to almost six full days away. Besides, as the medical director of the heart transplant service, he felt it was important to make at least a cameo appearance for the residents and the transplant coordinators, if not for the attending surgeons who were increasingly unavailable for morning rounds because of heightened demands to operate and generate revenue. It seemed like both surgical and medical doctors were under pressure to increase clinical income these days. Over the years, reimbursements from Medicare and private insurers declined steadily and the only way to make up for these cutbacks was to see more patients and do more surgeries.

This was a particularly bad time to provoke any new tensions between himself and Hurtuk. As inconceivable as it seemed to heart transplant doctors around the country and the world, Dan Ulek and Jack Hurtuk were each on the short-list of candidates for one of the most coveted positions in the world of organ transplantation — director of the Pittsburgh State Transplant Institute. The chances of identifying two individuals from the same institution for this prestigious position were small enough. That two of the top candidates for the position worked just two hours up the turnpike and across the Pennsylvania-Ohio line was also remarkable. That Pittsburgh was considering a non-surgeon like Ulek was even more amazing in the eyes of many in the field — particularly old-schoolers who felt that the surgical roots of solid organ transplantation mandated that surgeons fill all leadership positions.

As he rambled down Cedar Road viewing the Cleveland skyline five miles to the west, Dan erased all of these concerns and concentrated on plans for the afternoon flight to Paris. He loved to travel, especially to foreign countries. He loved big jets, business class seats, and first class service.

Arriving at his office at 7:20 a.m., he had time to check his Palm Pilot under the file he labeled "European Trips." Of course, he had to filter through the scattered papers and folders on his desktop to *find* his Palm Pilot. He was one of those people who simply couldn't work in a clean and organized environment. The messier his desk, the more productive he tended to be — another example of how he differed from his wife. Kathy kept her recipes and other important documents neatly filed in Tupperware boxes in the kitchen or den, and Dan was often devilishly tempted to "accidentally" dump one of the boxes on the floor just to test her fortitude.

He added "Paris, September 2001" and then counted thirteen trips to Europe since 1989. This was the fourth trip to Paris, one of his favorite cities. *What kind of strange bird would keep a list of trips overseas?* But he was proud of the list. Each of these trips was based on an invited talk, and the number of trips per year had increased dramatically in the past few years — a credit to his academic success and international recognition. Kathy also loved Europe and traveled with him for nine of those thirteen trips, also documented in the Palm Pilot file. When she came along, the excursions usually were extended for a few days of sightseeing, eating, drinking, and romancing. The romancing part always seemed better on the road than at home. Although Kathy often pointed out that she and Dan were complete opposites, love of travel turned out to be one of the few things that they had in common and that they nurtured over time.

But Kathy could not make today's trip. For one thing, she needed to stay behind to drive their oldest son, Tom, back to Ohio State for the fall semester. Besides, she would never travel to Europe for just two and half days — one and a half of which would be spent in airports or on airplanes — even though such trips were becoming routine for Dan. This trip to Paris was strictly business for Dan and perhaps the most important medical meeting of his life. He was invited to give the keynote address at the annual meeting of the International Heart Transplantation Society. *Not just a talk — the keynote address.* The talk itself would be easy — really just a review of ten years of clinical research on the prevention of chronic rejection in heart transplant recipients, focusing on immune monitoring and some of the newer immunosuppressive drugs. The importance of this otherwise routine talk was in the prestige — giving the *keynote* address at the most important international meeting in the field of heart transplantation. In Dan's mind, this might be the clincher in the competition for the Pittsburgh job. Interestingly, Jack Hurtuk decided not to attend the Paris meeting, citing a couple of overdue book chapters as an excuse. Dan knew it was a form of protest. In circles outside of the Cleveland Medical Center, Hurtuk made it clear that he was appalled that the society had asked a non-surgeon to give this year's address.

Dan led the team of nurses and residents into the ICU. Darlene May was doing poorly. She had received her heart transplant only seven months earlier and now was admitted with pneumonia complicated by respiratory and kidney failure. She was on a ventilator and receiving continuous veno-venous hemofiltration — a form of slow and continuous dialysis performed around the clock to replace the functions of her shut-down kidneys. Ironically, the function of her transplanted heart had been perfect prior to this devastating sequence of events. Undoubtedly, the pneumonia was exacerbated by the need for immunosuppressive drugs, which increase the risk and severity of infections — but that's the price that transplant recipients paid for the benefits of their new organs.

Dan figured that Darlene's chances of surviving were close to nil.

"Another death and graft loss in the first year after transplantation — we better be careful or we'll be looking at a UNOS site visit," Dan said to Deb half-jokingly and out of the earshot of the residents. UNOS — the United Network for Organ Sharing — was the government-hired agency that dictated organ allocation policies, maintained a national database for research purposes, and monitored programs for adverse outcomes. Auditing commit-tees from UNOS had the authority to recommend probationary measures for programs, either temporarily or permanently, if poor outcomes persisted for more than a short period of time. Outcomes at single centers — such as rates of patient and graft survival over one to five years — were regularly compared to national norms in order to identify outliers.

High volume and good outcomes were the holy grails of the transplant world. In the Ulek-Hurtuk era, both improved steadily, but there was a constant concern that pushing volume by accepting marginal recipients or marginal donors would yield inferior out-comes. Maintaining the balance was a source of constant stress, not to mention frequent debates about the acceptability of transplant candidates during bimonthly Recipient Committee Meetings.

After spending thirty minutes with Darlene, rounds proceed-ed smoothly and relatively quickly despite having patients on four different floors in the Tower. This month's residents were pretty sharp and were up to date on the clinical status of each patient, including the results of all recent laboratory tests and imaging studies. Good residents always made Dan's life easy. There was only one new admission from the night before and none of the current inpatients was ready to be discharged home. It was the new admissions and discharges that took up the most time on rounds, also accounting for more paperwork that needed to be completed later in the day. Dan figured he could dictate his one admission note in his office before noon and have plenty of time to get to the airport.

"Is Kathy going to Paris with you for some 'oo-la-la'?" asked Deb toward the end of rounds.

Dan loved Deb. She was a well-trained nurse practitioner — in her mid forties — and had been the inpatient transplant coor-dinator for more than eight years. Arguably, her level of knowledge and expertise in heart transplantation was as good as any doctor's. But she had much more direct contact with patients, who invari-ably loved her. One of her major responsibilities was to teach new transplant patients about the post-transplant routine: how to take their medications, when to come to the outpatient clinic for follow-up, who to call if they were sick or had questions. Compliance with the regimen was a key to a successful transplantation, and Deb was a superb patient educator. She was always on top of things and, much like his wife, was compulsively organized. Although the inpatient team was very dependent on the work of interns and residents, it was Deb who really ran the service. When he was the attending physician on the inpatient service, Dan simply provided oversight and also kept Deb up to date on the latest breakthroughs from meetings and journals.

Deb's question about Kathy once again removed Dan's mind from the daily rounding routine.

"No, this is a quick trip. I arrive in Paris tomorrow morning. My keynote address *(make sure she knows it is not just a simple talk, but a KEYNOTE address)* is three hours after I arrive and I return the next morning — just in time to talk to Renal about Darlene's CVVH orders later that afternoon. In the mean time, let's hold her tacrolimus until her kidneys show some signs of recovery and increase her methylprednisolone to 20 mg daily until we can restart the tacro."

"Got it." She nodded to the rounding intern. "I'll put the orders in for you. I don't know how you do it, Dan. I hope that Darlene is still with us when you get back. Have a safe trip."

"Oh, I will. Thanks, Deb."

I'm not sure how I do it either — I'll be a zombie giving that keynote address. He envisioned the routine. During the trip from Cleveland to Newark, he would fire up the laptop and review his PowerPoint slides for maybe the twentieth time. *Thirty minute presentation — a piece of cake.* The two-hour layover in Newark would allow a visit to the President's Club — plenty of time to recharge the laptop and have a couple of scotch-on-the-rocks. Once on the jumbo jet, he would have a glass of champagne, some roasted cashews, and 10 mg of Ambien. He would tell the flight attendant to skip dinner if he was sleeping — as he inevitably was: a perfectly legal state of unconsciousness. He *loved*

to travel. Under usual circumstances, upon arriving in Europe
— most often in the early morning — he would feel rejuvenated
but would check into the hotel and force himself to sleep till
mid-afternoon. For this trip, he would need to stay awake and
remain energized for his mid-morning talk.

Two

Valentine's Day —
February 1998

Dan and Kathy met Jack and Nancy Hurtuk for dinner. Over the preceding years, it had become a Valentine's Day tradition. The couples had become close acquaintances over the years and got together — usually for dinner at a restaurant — several times a year. They shared a common love for classic cocktails, gourmet food, and good wine.

"All human beings and all cultures share three common desires," Jack often said and reminded the others during appetizers. "Eating, screwing, and getting intoxicated. The eating and screwing parts are obviously essential for survival and procreation. The intoxication part is optional of course — could be alcohol, drugs, religious meditation —some means of altering consciousness." Like the other three people at the table, Jack was raised Catholic. But he was now an avowed agnostic, losing his religion when his parents died relatively young with less than optimal medical care — his father from lung cancer and mother from cirrhosis — each before they had turned sixty. Both parents suffered miserably before dying and Jack could not believe in any god that would allow such pain and misery. Dealing with dying parents as a young man was a big motivation for Jack's ultimate interest in a medical career.

Dan always hated when the subject of religion came up, especially in recent years, and quickly changed the subject. *If Jack is going to bring up religion, I'll bring up travel.*

"Well, that's why Kathy and I love to travel," said Dan. "Seeing how people in different parts of the world pursue those desires — eating, drinking, and . . . you know. As they say, 'travel is the enemy of bigotry' — you find that people in other parts of the world are more like us than unlike us."

Jack shrugged.

Dan went on, "By the way, why aren't you going to the conference in Florence next month? It should be a great international meeting and I hear that Florence is magnificent."

"I have an invited editorial that's overdue for the Journal of Heart Transplantation," said Jack. Dan knew that, in reality, Jack had not been invited.

Nancy excused herself to go to the ladies' room.

Jack and Nancy rarely traveled. She spent six months of her junior year in college in London, but inexplicably, Jack almost never traveled outside the country and had never been to Europe, despite numerous opportunities. For four years, he had served as a councilor on the Board of the American Transplantation Society, but often came up with excuses to avoid traveling to the board meetings. Many times, those excuses revolved around sick patients, and Dan respected Jack for that. Dan and his colleagues in cardiology had no problem covering each other's patients for out-of-town meetings or vacations. The same was true for many academic surgeons. Jack, on the other hand, had a deep sense of personal responsibility for patients that he operated on. Over the years, he would cancel many trips to meetings at the last minute because of a new transplant or because one of his patients had an unexpected postoperative complication. Although Jack had enjoyed a successful career as a surgeon, Dan believed that his success as an *academic* heart transplant surgeon probably had been stymied by his extraordinary devotion to his patients.

The pre-dinner conversation predictably shifted to the children, thanks to Kathy's intervention. She hated when dinner meetings involving doctors focused on professional matters, and she was artful and diplomatic at forcing a change to a subject that engaged all of the diners. Jack and Nancy's oldest child, Steven, was doing well in his junior year at Princeton. He was majoring in computer engineering and already had job offers from several companies in Silicon Valley. Their daughter, Susan, was captain of the girls' basketball team at Shaker Heights High School and was just accepted at Stanford. She hadn't made a final decision, awaiting news about a possible scholarship. She already had scholarship offers at Northwestern, the University of Virginia, and Dartmouth.

Dan and Kathy's oldest son, Tom, was a senior at Solon High School. He had applied only to state schools in Ohio, and to date, had been accepted at none of them. "He's thinking of pre-med," said Kathy, hoping to avoid the inevitable queries about which college he had chosen. Dan knew that she was stretching the truth. Tom hated his science and math courses in high school and his strongest ambition was to attend a college close to Cleveland to be close to his high school girlfriend. Dan figured that Tom's grades were good enough to get accepted at one of Ohio's state universities, but a major in pre-med was unlikely.

It was harmless to discuss the twins, Lauren and Brian, now in eighth grade.

"And how's Michael?" asked Nancy. "Still in remission?"

"It's been tough for him to catch up in school — he has missed almost a year and a half when you add it up — but physically, he's fine. God has answered all my prayers," said Kathy.

Jack flinched a bit but offered, "You guys really have survived an incredible ordeal. I'm not sure how you ever managed."

Kathy would have been delighted to spend more time talking about Michael's prolonged illness, but Dan quickly changed the subject to food as the waiter tried for the third time to take orders. The couples were fond of trying trendy restaurants and, for this occasion, chose *Lilac* — a new upscale place in Tremont advertising a fusion cuisine combining Mediterranean and new American dishes. It took two months to get a weekend reservation at the place, and for Valentine's Day, they had to settle for a five o'clock seating. It was obvious that the waiters were under orders to "roll 'em in and roll 'em out" to accommodate as many seatings as possible.

"Looks like an interesting menu. I'm starving," said Dan.

"This place reminds me of that old world restaurant near Wisconsin and M Street in Georgetown — what was it?" Jack asked.

"Old Europe," recalled Dan.

Memories of medical school reminded Dan of the disparate but intertwined paths that brought an academic cardiologist and an academic cardiothoracic surgeon to the same city, the same institution, and the same dinner table. Dan and Kathy were both natives of the Cleveland area. He met her when they were classmates at Loyola University in Chicago. They were from different parts of the Cleveland area — he from Solon and she from the southeast corner of the city wedged between Shaker and Warrensville Heights. They did not know each other before college. Both were majoring in pre-med through the first half of their sophomore year when they first met, but Kathy got frustrated after getting a C in organic chemistry and changed her major to dietetics.

Graduating summa cum laude, Dan wanted to attend a medical school on the east coast and, because of his Catholic roots, chose Georgetown over several Ivy League schools. He excelled in medical school. Surgery was the first of his clinical rotations in the third year. He loved it. He loved the long hours and loved the sanctuary-like state of being in an operating room. He especially loved even the miniscule amounts of sewing and cutting allotted to a third year medical student.

"Doing something with my hands," he would offer in earlier years when his father would ask what he wanted to do with his life. However, his faculty mentor at Georgetown — a pathologist and assistant dean of the School of Medicine — met with Dan early in his third year and encouraged him to choose internal medicine instead of surgery. "The best and brightest students choose internal medicine or psychiatry. Surgery is for trade school dummies."

Jack Hurtuk was a native of Boston and also attended medical school at Georgetown after graduating from Boston College. Strangely, Dan and Jack barely knew each other during their four years at Georgetown. The medical school class was relatively large, and students often formed small social circles, many times consisting of groups with the same clinical rotation schedules, with separate rotations in surgery, internal medicine, pediatrics, Ob-Gyn, and neurology. With rotations at nine different affiliated hospitals in the Maryland-D.C.-Virginia area, it was quite possible to spend the last two years of medical school mingling with only a handful of fellow students. Dan's social circle consisted of a group of students who lived close to each other in apartments in Arlington, Virginia — just across the Potomac River from D.C. He could barely afford sharing rent with two other students in a humble Arlington abode up the hill from the Pentagon. Jack's father was a successful journalist and an editor for the Boston Globe. When each of his parents died at a relatively young age, Jack and his older brother inherited enough money to cover their educations. Jack went through medical school with relative affluence, living in the second floor apartment of a Georgetown townhouse, a short walking distance to the medical campus and close to the lively restaurants and pubs of the Georgetown area.

Ironically, Dan remembered sitting next to Jack and his attractive brunette girlfriend in the auditorium on "Match Day" — the early spring day when senior medical students discover which residency program they would be attending based on a computerized system that matched the wish lists of the candidates with those of the residency programs. It was an interesting event with some deliriously happy and pleasantly surprised students — and others who left the auditorium grossly disappointed. For Dan, the process was a bit tedious as he was expecting no personal surprise. And the fact that names were called in alphabetical order made for a long afternoon. He recalled Hurtuk's cry of joy when Jack learned that he matched in Surgery at the Massachusetts General Hospital in Boston. He leaned over and gave his girlfriend a long kiss. *Not bad for a trade school dummy. He's going to Harvard.* "Congratulations, man. And good luck at Mass General," Dan offered. He was green with envy.

As expected, Dan matched in Internal Medicine at Ohio State. In fact, he listed only two programs in the match: OSU and a safety — Georgetown itself — having been promised a position if he chose to stay there. During medical school, he was highly regarded during all of his clinical rotations and assisted a cardiologist at the Washington Hospital Center with a research project that ultimately resulted in co-authorship of a manuscript published in the Annals of Internal Medicine — no small feat for a medical student — and something that stimulated his interest in cardiology. Secretly, he had hoped to apply for one of the prestigious residencies in the northeast or on the west coast. But Kathy had returned to the Cleveland area after college and, following completion of a one-year internship in dietetics, was working as a dietician at a community hospital in Bedford. For four years, she had maintained a long-distance relationship with Dan, exchanging travel back and forth between Cleveland and D.C. She wanted him to return to Ohio as they had planned their wedding at the end of his internship year. She moved to Columbus after the wedding and lived there with Dan for two years before moving back to Cleveland where Dan landed a fellowship in cardiology at the CMC.

The appetizers at Lilac were great — especially Dan's seared fois gras and Nancy's soft-shelled crab. None of the entrees were quite as impressive. *Why don't I order three courses of appetizers and skip the entrees at places like this?* Jack, an oenophile with an enormous wine cellar in his basement at home, ordered two excellent bottles of red wine with dinner — vertical samplings of two Heitz Cellars cabernet sauvignons — after an earlier round of manhattans and martinis. Dan and Kathy always marveled at Jack's mastery of the wine lingo — "great legs, good nose, great complexity, nice acidity, subtle blackberry finish." For Dan, it just tasted good. And knowing wine was easy: the more expensive the bottle, the better the wine. Kathy was not a big fan of red wine and remained sober enough to drive home later. By the time coffee and dessert arrived, Dan and Jack were pleasantly drunk and, as usual, turned the conversation back from family to work.

"It's hard to believe that in just a decade and a half, we've grown the program from being almost nonexistent to being the third largest heart program in the country," said Jack. "We are the dynamic duo, my friend. We both deserve awards of some kind — master surgeon and master cardiologist. Sometimes I wonder if there is anything more to achieve."

I hope he isn't drunk enough to go into his "I've mastered surgery – only golf remains to be conquered" routine.

"Don't take this the wrong way, Dan, but sometimes I feel like there is little else for me to accomplish in cardiothoracic surgery. I really would like Jeff Schick's job. I could be department chair and continue to operate — maybe cut down to ten or fifteen transplants a year. I still love the operating room, but I'd stop harvesting the organs and give all that middle-of-the-night stuff to the junior guys and surgical fellows. I could focus more on research and writing."

"I'm sure you'll be chairman some day, Jack. But don't be in a hurry. The program has been successful largely because of your surgical skills and leadership and I'm not sure if Rob or Mark could keep up without you," said Dan, referring to Jack's two junior surgical partners. As much as he hated cowering to Jack's large ego, he respected him as an excellent doctor and a remarkably talented surgeon. "If I ever need coronary bypass surgery or a transplant, I want you around."

"Yeah, yeah — well, maybe a five-year plan. I'm not getting any younger," said Jack, stifling a yawn. Although they graduated from the same medical school class, Jack was five years older than Dan, having embarked upon a career in journalism — taking after his father — before making the jump to medicine. "Guess none of us are getting any younger. Although you two lovely ladies sure look good tonight! Tab's on us this time. We really need to do this more often. Good food and good company. See you on rounds in the morning."

"Can never decide if I love him or hate him," Dan said to Kathy during their drive home. "And I think he was staring at your boobs halfway through the second bottle of red wine."

For years, Kathy had listened to Dan and other cardiologists tell stories about Jack's emotional volatility and hot-tempered behavior at work — constantly threatening to fire residents and fellows, screaming on rounds when he hadn't been notified in a timely fashion about some adverse patient outcome, and throwing instruments in the operating room. But from a social point of view, she always found him to be kind and polite, mildly egomaniacal, and pleasantly flirtatious.

"Jack was just being Jack. I had a wonderful night, Dan. I am so proud of both of you. And at least someone was paying attention to my boobs!"

Three

Columbus, Ohio — 1979

Kathy landed a job as a staff dietician at Riverside Hospital, making more than twice Dan's salary as a resident at Ohio State's University Hospital. He was on call every third night and every third weekend. In their early months in Columbus, Kathy frequently felt lonely. Regular phone calls to her mother back in Cleveland helped, but the long distance bills limited those interactions. They had a one bedroom apartment with almost no furniture. Dan's parents bought them a bedroom set as a wedding gift. The living room contained only a thirty-year-old couch that was shedding stuffing, and an aging black-and-white television with a nineteen-inch screen. Kathy's sister gave them an old kitchen table, but they had no real chairs and used two stools to sit down for their meals. The only good news was that they were well-stocked in the kitchen, thanks to shower and wedding gifts — the perfect young couple — proud owners of three blenders and two food processors. They had a complete set of china for a party of eight — just no place to serve the guests.

Tom was conceived in Columbus less than three months after their wedding and Kathy was a little embarrassed to tell the Riverside Dietetics Department a few months later that she would need to take a maternity leave so shortly after beginning her job. She had terrible morning sickness during her first trimester, often dealing with it while her new husband was away on-call at the hospital. She now understood why trainees in medicine were called *residents* — because they literally *lived* in the hospital for long periods of time. Those early days in Columbus provided a training ground for her life as a doctor's wife. She quickly became accustomed to missed dinners, holidays alone, cancelled reservations, and phones ringing in the middle of the night. All of this was magnified after Tom's birth. She was willing to change all of the diapers and handle all of the baths, but sharing "baby call" at night was not possible when Dan himself was on-call at the hospital. Aside from taking care of Tom, Kathy utilized her time alone by reading (at least one novel a week) and by keeping the apartment meticulously clean. No matter what time of the day or night Dan returned from the hospital, the place was spotless.

Dan's internship and residency at Ohio State marked the end of a long chain of education and training at Catholic institutions. For grade school, it was St. Henry's for the early years and later St. Rita's when his parents moved to Solon. For high school, it was Walsh Jesuit; then it was Loyola University for college and Georgetown University for medical school. It all reflected his Slovak-Hungarian ethnicity and strict Catholic family traditions — rules and traditions that he began questioning as a teenager. *No meat on Fridays? I prefer shrimp anyhow. Do I really burn in hell if I miss one Sunday Mass? Unwanted children are preferred to using a condom?*

Kathy was raised in an Irish family also with strict Catholic rules. She continued to go to Mass, not just on Sundays but even on the holy days of obligation, many of which Dan had forgotten long ago. Whenever he was not on-call, he would go to church with Kathy on Sundays and on religious holidays — but he realized that he was doing it more for her than for himself.

Although Kathy would have loved being a full-time mom, she needed to return to work after her three-month maternity leave to keep the household financially solvent. Fortunately, she befriended an older couple on their apartment floor. They were in their late fifties or early sixties. Their two children were grown and gone, and the wife, Marsha, was happy to babysit Tom during the days for a little extra income. On many days when Kathy returned from work in the late afternoon, Marsha would invite her to stay for a cup of tea. Marsha rarely spent any time away from her apartment or her husband, so she was delighted to spend some time chatting with another woman, even one who was much younger. Kathy also enjoyed these afternoon chats and would share stories about husbands, families, birthdays, anniversaries, first communions, and deaths. Marsha and her husband were both Russian immigrants, speaking with fairly thick accents — and Kathy enjoyed learning about Russian customs, comparing them to those derived from her own Irish heritage.

"Tom is such a good baby. He's going to need a playmate or two soon. Are you and Dan thinking about having more children?"

"I'd love to have five or six, but Dan is already thinking about college tuition and keeps saying that two kids are plenty. My guess is that it will turn out to be somewhere in between."

"You're lucky to have such a compromising husband! And so handsome. But for Christmas, I want to buy him a new pair of shoes."

Kathy was startled by the comment, but realized that her Russian friend was guilty only of brutal honesty. High fashion was not one of Dan's strengths. In fact, he never expressed any interest in new clothes. He would wear the same pair of brown shoes, day after day, month after month, until he wore holes into the soles. At any point in time, he would have two or maybe three favorite shirts and would ask Kathy to wash them two or three times a week so he could wear them over and over again. He would sometimes wear the same trousers for two weeks in a row and changed socks no more than weekly. Kathy constantly offered to buy him new clothes, but he refused to let her buy clothes that he didn't try on first — and of course he never found the time to go shopping.

She often scolded him. "I know we're not rich but you don't need to look like a bum. You're a doctor for crying out loud. You can afford a new suit and a nice pair of leather shoes."

She smiled at Marsha as she finished her tea. "Marsha, my dear, you are a very perceptive woman! But please spend your money on something more important than Dan's shoes. Dan is my problem. All mine. I've learned to take the bad with the good. My mother has always been fond of saying 'never try to change the man you marry — that's the secret to a healthy marriage.' I think she is probably right."

Marsha glanced over at her husband who was napping and intermittently snoring on the living room couch. She looked back at Kathy knowingly, and smiled in agreement. "See you tomorrow — same time, same place."

Between paying for child care and Dan's paltry house staff salary, it was difficult to make ends meet in those early years. But Kathy and Dan were not totally devoid of a social life. They found a lovely and inexpensive Mexican restaurant just south of the OSU campus, serving authentic Mexican dishes. On Friday evenings, when Dan was not on call, Marsha would keep Tom for a few extra hours. Dan and Kathy would feast on margaritas, red sangria, chips and hot salsa, mole poblano, carne asada, or beef enchiladas. They were poor as paupers, but they were happy as hell.

Toward the end of his second year of residency, the chief of the Department of Medicine at Ohio State called Dan for a meeting and invited him to serve a fourth year as a chief resident after he completed his three year residency. Being a chief resident was considered to be prestigious and often provided the platform for an academic career. But Dan had intended to extend his training with a fellowship — hopefully in cardiology — after completing his residency and was already in the process of submitting applications, mostly to academic medical centers in Ohio. Fellowship training programs for most sub-specialties, including cardiology, were three years in duration. If he accepted the offer to serve as chief resident, that would be seven years of training, in addition to four years of medical school. He would be almost thirty-three years old before he was ready for a *real* job. Unlike many of his friends who came from families of affluence, Dan and Kathy both started with humble family backgrounds and he felt the need to get on with establishing a family life that was better than either he or Kathy had known as children. His performance throughout his residency years was outstanding and he believed he already had the credentials to embark upon an academic career. After long discussions with Kathy, he turned down the offer to be chief resident.

He applied to five cardiology fellowship programs, all in Ohio, knowing that any of them would be within reasonable driving distance from friends and family in the Cleveland area. Kathy was delighted — and not surprised — when Dan matched at his first choice, the Cleveland Medical Center. She would miss Marsha and her chats over tea, but she was excited about returning to the Cleveland area. She didn't care if it was the *Mistake on the Lake* or *Home of the Burning River.* She and Dan were going home.

Four

Cleveland Heights, Ohio —
1983

Life was pleasant in those early days back in Cleveland. Tom was almost two years old and Kathy was five months' pregnant with Michael and beginning to show. She was so happy to be back home. Her parents still lived in the southeast section of Cleveland. They had refused to flee during the "white flight" of the early 1960s and were content living in a racially integrated, but mostly African-American, neighborhood. Kathy and her older brother were afraid to visit in anything but broad daylight — and constantly encouraged their parents to consider a move to the suburbs. Shortly after the move back to Cleveland, Kathy's mother developed ovarian cancer. She survived for more than three years before succumbing to a related bowel obstruction. Kathy was forever thankful to be nearby in her mother's time of need.

When they moved back to Cleveland from Columbus, Dan insisted on living in a suburb that was a short driving distance to the CMC. They mostly looked at close-in suburbs like Shaker Heights and Cleveland Heights to the east, and Lakewood to the west. Their first home in Cleveland Heights was a perfect starter — a three-bedroom colonial within a fifteen minute drive to CMC, a ten minute drive to Kathy's parents, twenty-five minutes to Dan's parents in Solon, and within walking distance to St. Ann's Catholic Church. Dan's academic salary was less than he could make in private practice, but it was still almost twice the combined salaries that he and Kathy generated during their last year in Columbus. Relatively speaking, it seemed like they were rich.

Dan had finished his fellowship at CMC and was an obvious choice for recruitment to the faculty. As a fellow, he was an excellent teacher and was loved by medical students, interns, and residents. He wanted a career centered on teaching and research, rather than one in which he would be buried in the cardiac catheterization lab — fully aware that he was moving away from *procedural* medicine *("doing something with my hands")* and more toward *cognitive* medicine. After his first year on the faculty, Rick Weichel — who was recruited from Yale to be chief of the Cardiology Division at CMC a year before Dan joined the faculty — asked him to serve as the division's fellowship training program director. He was happy to take on the new responsibilities. He was only a year out of his own fellowship, but he enjoyed mentoring younger trainees. Aside from his teaching and training director responsibilities, Dan was busy building a large academic practice. Patients loved him and that helped to build a growing referral base of local community internists and family practitioners.

After one year on the faculty, however, he was not involved in research of any kind and certainly had generated no publications. He often wondered whether he could have developed a more robust research career if he had stayed to be chief resident at Ohio State. As a fellow, he had participated in some chart review studies and published two case reports, but he was hoping to embark on a long-term research study of some kind and realized that he had no suitable mentor within the division. He also was worried about the old academic axiom — *publish or perish* — and met with Weichel for advice.

"The old academic paradigm has changed and these days we have a need for faculty members who focus on patient care and teaching," said Weichel.

"But how do I get promoted at Case Western Reserve University for patient care and teaching?"

Rick really liked Dan whose ambition and raw love of medicine reminded Rick of himself in the early part of his career. "The latest rules require only that you have recognized teaching skills and either regional or national recognition to be promoted from assistant to associate professor of medicine."

"And so how does one achieve national recognition?" asked Dan.

They were both thinking the same thing: research and publications. It was the *Catch 22* of academic medicine — all academic medical centers wanted clinical faculty members devoted to patient care in order to generate clinical revenue, but were unwilling to honor them with promotion unless they performed research that generated publication in highly cited journals.

"I'm happy for now, Kath," Dan noted one night while rubbing Kathy's pregnant belly. "But if some research prospects don't materialize in the next year or two, I may need to bust a move."

"Why can't you be happy doing what you are doing now? You're a good doctor and a good teacher, and you're making more money than we've ever seen before."

Dan paused to think. "I'm not sure if I'll *ever* be completely happy. I'll always want more, want to do it all, and want to be the best." Throughout the early portions of his career, Dan never ceased to be amazed by the giants of medicine and surgery — most often department chairs or division chiefs at major academic medical centers — who had moved from one city to another to climb the ladder. Rick Weichel was just one of many examples, having worked at three other centers before moving to Cleveland to become a division chief. Dan wondered whether a move to a new center in a new city was *essential* to being truly successful in his field.

The baby started kicking and Dan giggled and kissed his wife's modestly protruding belly, then fell asleep at her side. Kathy stayed awake. She was perfectly happy with Dan and their new family, but she was worried about their future. She and Dan were classic examples of opposites being attracted to each other. They had almost nothing in common. He liked classic rock and roll; she preferred Motown. He was a sports fanatic; she could care less. He loved science fiction movies; she hated them. She loved surprise parties; he didn't understand the point. She wanted six children; he was already talking about a vasectomy. She loved the change of seasons; he could take twelve months on the beach. Then there was always the discussion about living somewhere other than Cleveland.

She wondered if opposites could attract forever.

One day a few weeks later, Dan came home gleaming — carrying a box of red roses in his arms. Rick Weichel had called Dan for a meeting and offered him a 6 percent increase in salary for the next academic year. Rick apparently sensed that Dan was frustrated by the lack of research and publications, and he wanted to assure him that he was a valued member of the division and the Department of Medicine. Dan was elated. After the new baby was born, he wanted to look for a bigger new home in southern Cuyahoga County — maybe Walton Hills or Solon. They were going to need more space for their growing family. Kathy's concerns were allayed for the time being and she would be delighted with a bigger house, still reasonably close to her parents. After dinner, she put Tom to bed and invited Dan to the master bedroom, offering him a big wet kiss to get things started. Life was good.

Five

Boston, Massachusetts —
1984

It was after midnight and Nancy ordered a glass of champagne at a piano bar on Beacon Street in Brookline. During their days in Boston, this had become a favorite place for Jack and Nancy to end special evenings. For their anniversary, Jack made reservations at the Bay Tower Room, a "penthouse" restaurant atop one of Boston's Government Center skyscrapers, offering beautiful views of Quincy Market and the North End. The piano bar was three blocks from their Brookline apartment, offering a perfect place for after-dinner drinks and a drunken walk home.

"Champagne at this hour? Yuk," said Jack, favoring cognac or single malt bourbons as his after dinner drinks of choice. He disliked champagne at any hour but figured, at best, it was a pre-dinner drink for New Year's Eve or other special holidays.

"Hey, maybe I'm just getting started," Nancy retaliated with a sparkle in her eye, realizing that, in fact, the night was close to an end.

It was one of the many quirks that Jack had learned to live with since marrying Nancy during his third year of residency at Mass General. He met her during his senior year at Georgetown. She was a native of Detroit. After graduating from Wayne State she moved to D.C. to work as a paralegal, hoping to apply to law school eventually. To make ends meet, she ultimately needed a second job as a waitress and met Jack while working at *The Tombs*, a pub-grub favorite of Georgetown students — conveniently located in the basement of the much less affordable *1789*, a French restaurant in the heart of Georgetown. Nancy moved in to live with Jack in his Georgetown townhouse during the last half of his senior year, and followed him to Boston.

The piano player was alternating between Barry Manilow and Beatles tunes, and Jack knew he had drunk too much when he caught himself singing along. He looked at Nancy and asked himself if he had made the right choice in marrying her. During college and medical school, he was a serious womanizer and friends would constantly encourage him to slow down — to get a life. Nancy was probably the first woman who refused to have sex with Jack after two dates. He was angry, intrigued, and more determined than ever to win her over — ultimately succeeding. Nancy was madly in love with Jack and was more than happy to move to Boston with him when he finished medical school. She had given up on the idea of law school. Marrying a Harvard-trained surgeon was a very appealing alternative.

One thing that Nancy and Jack had in common was the lack of parents, all four of them having died at relatively young ages. Nancy had two older married sisters living in Chicago and northeast Ohio. She kept in touch by way of telephone calls every few months, but was able to visit each sister no more than once a year — usually for holiday get-togethers. Jack's only sibling was his older brother Jerry, a neurosurgeon who trained at the University of California in San Francisco before going into private practice in the East Bay area. He was eight years older than Jack, graduated from college before Jack started high school, had been married and divorced twice, and almost never communicated with his kid brother.

Nancy got pregnant during Jack's second year of residency, and a Boston judge quietly married them with no more than a handful of friends in attendance.

The piano player was singing "Copacabana" as Jacked stared at Nancy sipping her champagne. *Do I love her? Have I ever really loved her? Will I be with her forever?* As always, it was their children — now six and four years old — who kept the marriage going. Nancy quit working when Steven was born and became a remarkably good full-time mom. During his residency years, Jack's call schedule was outrageous — he was on every other weekend. During the week, he was often called in to help with emergencies even when he was technically "off". Nancy never complained. *She really has been a good wife and a great mother.*

"So how did you like the Bay Tower Room?" asked Jack. "I thought the food was great and the wine list was incredible."

"The food was great and those views of the Boston harbor were fantastic," she replied.

"Would you put it on your list of Boston favorites?" he asked.

"I'm still partial to the historical places — you know, like the Union Oyster House or Locke Ober — but it's certainly up there on my list of top-of-the-town restaurants. It was a great choice for an anniversary dinner, Jack."

"So do you really like Boston?" asked Jack.

Nancy could tell this was a loaded question. They had been living in the Boston area for seven years. Both of their children were born at St. Margaret's Women's Hospital. After Steven was born, they moved from a one-bedroom apartment in Cambridge to a larger two-bedroom apartment in Brookline, close to everything, thanks to the Green Line segment of Boston's "T". She liked the European flavor of the city and its proximity to the mountains of New Hampshire and the beaches of Cape Cod. Jack was now a full-time faculty member at Harvard and the Mass General and, although his schedule was still demanding, their life style had improved dramatically compared to those hectic years when he was a surgical resident. She *loved* Boston and felt like they were just now beginning to settle down.

"Well, it's no Detroit — but yeah, I like it here. Why are you asking? I thought you liked Boston, too."

"Oh, I love the area. I'm just not sure if we can afford to live here forever."

"Jack, we just dropped one hundred sixty bucks at a fabulous restaurant, not to mention parking and whatever we'll owe the babysitter. We're living in an upscale section of Brookline. You just joined the faculty three years ago. It seems like we are doing okay."

"It's all relative, Nancy. Do you realize that Jerry makes more than six times my salary out in the Bay area?"

"He's older, and from what you've told me, probably dreadfully unhappy."

"That's not the point. The point is that the cost of living in Boston is very high but salaries in academic surgery are paradoxically low compared to other parts of the country. It may take years before we can afford to move into a house or even a larger apartment."

He thought that these latter comments would strike home. Nancy had been talking about a third child for some time and surely would understand that their current apartment would be too small for three growing kids. However, she seemed unfazed. The fact was that money had nothing to do with Jack's concerns about staying in Boston. He still had a large portion of his inheritance in bank accounts that Nancy didn't even know about. They could easily afford a sizable home on the north shore or in Newton or Wellesley. But Jack had no intention of staying in Boston. It was not about money. It was about ascending to a throne.

As a news editor for the health section of the Globe, Jack's father became very connected with the medical intelligentsia that congregated within the Boston city limits. From Joe Hurtuk's perspective, leaders in academic medicine accrued a great deal of power and money and were among the most influential people in the community. He himself had come from a medical family. His father and two uncles were general practitioners who settled in or around Portland, Maine. His own father was somewhat disappointed when his only son chose a nonmedical career. Although he had a very successful career as a journalist and editor, he was determined to steer his children toward careers in medicine. Much as Joseph Kennedy prepped his sons to be presidential candidates, Joe Hurtuk decided early during his sons' lives that they would be prominent physicians or surgeons. Jack remembered hearing the lectures as early as grade school: "Go to medical school and become a surgeon — that's where the money is; that's where the glory is."

Joe died before either of his sons went to medical school. He was a three-pack-a-day smoker and paid the price for his habit at the age of fifty-seven, dying a painful death. He would have been disappointed to know that Jerry opted for a career in private practice rather than in academics. Jack felt compelled to honor his father's wishes and to climb the ladder of academic surgery: assistant professor, associate professor, full professor. division chief, department chair, and — who knows – maybe even the dean of a medical school some day. But it wasn't going to happen at the Mass General. Jack was keenly interested in abdominal organ transplantation, but there were six surgeons of higher rank with the same interest and it was unlikely that he would surpass any of them in his drive to the top. On the other hand, he knew that the Harvard logo could serve as his ticket to a leadership position in a number of other academic medical centers in other parts of the country. *Okay Dad, it's not Harvard but I am the chair of the department!* From his point of view, neither he nor Nancy had family connections to tie them down to any particular city or state. *They* were free to move wherever *he* wanted.

In his first two years on the staff at Mass General, Jack quickly earned the reputation of being a surgeon's surgeon. His seemed to have innate surgical skills, best described by colleagues as *robotic* — no wasted movements, extremely fast and efficient. He had excellent outcomes with a low rate of surgical complications. Unfortunately, *surgical* skills were less important than *academic* skills when it came to promotion in the Harvard system. In contrast to many of his senior colleagues, Jack had no desire to be a basic scientist. Without funding from the National Institutes for Health to do scientific research, it could take Jack many years — even decades — to make the jump from assistant to associate professor of surgery. He was driven to succeed at a faster pace. It was a good time to consider a professional move, but he didn't think it was necessary to share his real motivations with his wife.

"Listen, Nancy, the salaries for academic surgeons are much higher in other cities — especially in the Midwest. If we want to consider living in a house instead of an apartment, I think I should start looking at opportunities in other parts of the country."

She could tell by the nature of the conversation that he already had.

She finished her champagne and put on her overcoat, signaling the end of the evening. As they walked back to their apartment, Nancy pondered their marriage. She loved Jack but was uncertain about his love for her. She did not enjoy playing a submissive role, but worried about how Jack would react if she vehemently rejected the idea of a move away from Boston. *If we are going to move, we might as well do it before Steven and Susan get too far along in school.* As they entered their apartment to greet the babysitter, she realized that they would be leaving soon, like it or not.

Six

Cleveland Medical Center —
1985

Dan got to his office and checked his calendar for the day. He was scheduled to see patients in clinic all morning, had a teaching conference at noon, and then was scheduled to interview Jack Hurtuk at 1:00 p.m. Hurtuk was now an assistant professor of surgery at Harvard and was in Cleveland interviewing for the position as chief of the Division of Heart Transplantation. At the time, Dan was also an assistant professor, of medicine, at Case Western Reserve University and was practicing general cardiology at CMC. Since joining the faculty in 1982, he had hoped to begin a clinical research program, maybe focused on treatment of heart failure, but he had trouble identifying a research mentor and was busy enough seeing patients. CMC had a fledgling heart transplant program, having performed four in the preceding year. There were no designated transplant cardiologists, and everyone got their chance to care for the handful of transplant recipients when they were attending on the inpatient cardiology service. Dan had been called by the chief of surgery who asked him to interview Hurtuk during his first recruitment visit, having heard that they were both Georgetown graduates and former classmates.

Jack walked into his office looking unchanged from his days in medical school. He was six feet tall, thin, and clean-shaven with a full head of wavy, reddish-brown hair. He had perfect teeth and a Kennedy-like smile. He always dressed impeccably, now wearing a suede sport coat, dark brown corduroy trousers, a light pink shirt with cuff links, and a paisley tie.

"Welcome to Cleveland, Jack. Looks like you've done well at MGH — always good to see another successful Hoya."

"Thanks. Georgetown seems just like yesterday, doesn't it?"

"So, why would you ever want to move to Cleveland? Boston's a great city and you can't beat Harvard."

"Yeah, I actually grew up on the south shore of Boston in Cohasset, but my parents have been dead for some time now and there really is no family left in the area. The lure here is a chance to be a program director. At MGH, there are too many people ahead of me and I don't see any of them moving anywhere in the near future. My wife and I do love Boston — we live in Brookline — but it's incredibly expensive and academic salaries are about 40 percent less than what you guys see out here in the Midwest. We'd be stuck in an apartment for another ten years. Besides, my wife, Nancy, has family in the Great Lakes area — including a sister who lives here in Mentor."

Our career paths always seem to be dictated by our spouses. But somehow I don't think Nancy's sister is high on his list of reasons to move to Cleveland. Dan's quick assessment was that Hurtuk was another Weichel-type — willing and able to move anywhere, anytime to increase his chances of promotion and success.

"But the heart transplant program here at CMC is tiny —
three or four transplants a year, max."

"Not that much smaller than any of the Boston heart programs.
Besides, all of that's going to change with cyclosporine."

Dan had cursorily read only a couple of papers about the
new immunosuppressive drug, but was reluctant to admit his
lack of knowledge. "I thought cyclosporine was associated with
lymphoma pretty routinely?"

"Always a learning curve with any new drug or therapy
— you know, dose finding, learning to manage toxicities. Keep
your eye on the transplant literature — the kidney trials are going to look very impressive. The world of cardiothoracic transplantation is going to be only a few steps behind."

Dan thought that Jack was either visionary or crazy.

Jack went on, "You know UNOS is soon going to mandate
an officially designated medical director for every approved
transplant program." Dan was only vaguely aware of UNOS and
he was too embarrassed to ask what the initials stood for.

"Is there anybody here that would qualify to be a medical
director?" asked Jack.

"Well no one person more than any another — we all take
our turns caring for the small number of transplant patients. The
cardiac management is pretty straightforward. Every time I'm
on service and have a transplant recipient in the house, I have to
re-learn the immunosuppression, but it's mostly remembering
the doses of azathioprine and prednisone."

"If I accept the job here, I'm going to demand that the Division of Cardiology name a medical director. It might as well be
you my friend. Give it some thought, especially if you have any
interest in doing clinical research — the opportunities for long-
term studies are going to be enormous."

Wow, did that strike a chord.

"There's a conference called the First International Cyclosporine Symposium being held in Houston next month. You
should ask your division chief to cough up a few bucks and send
you there."

"I just might do that."

As he escorted Jack out of his office for his next interview, Dan found himself again admiring his visitor's wardrobe. He looked down at his own shoes and noticed a hole on the outside of his right Hush Puppy. He shuffled sideways so Jack wouldn't notice.

During Hurtuk's second recruitment visit a month later, the chief of surgery arranged for a group meeting between Hurtuk, Rick Weichel, and all of the other staff cardiologists. Hurtuk gave a short research presentation — summarizing the Mass General experience with cyclosporine in animals and in early human trials. He then took time to present some of his visions for the CMC program — increased number of transplants, recruitment of new surgeons and cardiologists, new research programs — all the usual stuff that new recruits are supposed to promise. "In the realm of immunosuppression, I'm prepared to begin a protocol in which we will eliminate steroids and substitute cyclosporine."

That raised more than a few eyebrows in the room. Transplant patients all hated the side effects of steroids, but these drugs were the mainstay of immunosuppression since the early days of solid organ transplantation and had always been part of the CMC heart transplant protocol. *Visionary or crazy?*

He went on to describe UNOS and the evolving mandates for surgical and medical directorships for each organ transplant program.

Rick Weichel chimed in, "We might have to recruit someone for that job, unless someone already working here is willing to consider on-the-job training." Most of the other eyes in the room drifted downward.

Dan raised his hand and said, "I'll do it."

Jack accepted the job after a third visit and moved to the CMC officially three months later in early 1986. He was an excellent surgeon, as all the reference letters from Mass General had suggested. He also had excellent writing skills — probably reflecting his early years in journalism. Jack taught Dan a great deal about writing in general, particularly about writing medical manuscripts. Within two years, they had accumulated the country's largest experience with the use of cyclosporine in heart transplant recipients and had co-authored eight manuscripts published in high impact medical and surgical journals.

By 1988, the service was performing twenty heart transplants a year, and the prospects for further growth were excellent. Out-of-state patient referrals were becoming a big part of their program. Patients were willing to live in the Cleveland area for months or even years in order to be available for the chance to receive their heart transplant at the CMC. Hurtuk and Ulek were putting the program on the map. The two were becoming renowned, not only for their novel immunosuppression protocols, but also for developing a program that optimized patient care and made the center profitable. Just as often as Dan was being invited to give talks on cyclosporine, he was being invited as a consultant by hospital systems interested in starting up new transplant programs.

All was good.

Seven

Orlando, Florida — 1990

After another snowy winter, and suffering from his perennial case of cabin fever, Dan decided to begin the tradition of taking Kathy and the kids on a spring vacation. The twins had just turned five and probably were capable of lasting at least a few hours at the Magic Kingdom before pooping out and getting cranky. Tom and Michael were probably old enough to enjoy Epcot Center. Dan and Kathy realized that this "vacation" would be as much work as play for them, but they still looked forward to a change of scenery and warmer weather.

Dan booked adjoining rooms at the Dolphin Hotel, near the back entrance of Epcot. He had actually been to the hotel twice before for medical meetings and each time could not think of a poorer choice for a meeting of adults. First of all, the place was filled with screaming kids running up and down hallways and escalators. Secondly, the architect of this place either had childlike fantasies or, more likely, was using mind-altering drugs when designing the hotel. For example, the towering dolphins adorning the exterior corners of the hotel clearly had the markings of scales on their bodies and tails. Obviously, the architect did not realize that dolphins are not fish. Inside, the lobby of the hotel was a cacophony of bright lights and wildly contrasting colors. The walls of the main floors were covered with colorful wallpapers displaying everything from beach scenes to Disney characters. Dan had forewarned Kathy that the Dolphin would be no Ritz-Carlton.

But, as he expected, it was a fun place for the kids. A door connected Dan and Kathy's room with its king-size bed to the adjacent room with two doubles — plenty of space for the four young children to sleep. This was almost certainly the first time that any of the kids had slept in strange beds, all together in one room, with their *own* TV and bathroom. Frolicking in that hotel room was undoubtedly as much fun as meeting Mickey Mouse and Donald Duck in the Magic Kingdom.

They had planned four nights and five days. They visited the parks each morning and then brought the kids back to the hotel pool each afternoon. Although the pool's occupants were mostly children, Kathy enjoyed sitting in the water as quietly as possible, reading a novel, and sipping on a strawberry dai-quiri. *Some day I'd like a big house with an in-ground pool.* On two evenings, Kathy called for a hotel babysitter, so that she and Dan could go downstairs to find the closest thing to an adult bar as there was in the Dolphin. The babysitter was hardly necessary as the kids were all sound asleep each night by 8:00 p.m.

Sipping on his scotch-on-the-rocks, Dan's attention shifted back and forth from his wife to the porcelain statue of an ill-defined reptilian creature with a Cheshire cat grin on its face, just outside the pub's entrance.

"I told you this place would be wild. The kids seem to be having a great time, though. Tomorrow is Sunday. Have you asked if there's a Catholic church nearby?" Dan asked.

"We don't have to go to Mass when we are on vacation," she replied.

Dan was a bit dumbfounded. "Oh, really? When did that rule change?"

"It's no rule. I just think that there are times when family is more important than Sunday Mass."

They had been married for almost twelve years, but Dan was still learning about his wife's habits, rules, desires, and ambitions. He wondered if other married men had the same difficulties in knowing and understanding their wives. Religion was always a contentious issue. Kathy portrayed herself as a strict Catholic, but always had a way of bending rules of the Catholic Church to fit her lifestyle. Premarital sex was okay, so long as it was with the partner you planned to marry. Birth control was acceptable so long as you were planning on having children *eventually*. Confession wasn't necessary so long as you prayed to God each week at Mass. And now, the "no Mass necessary on vacation" rule.

This vacation served to put a lot of things into perspective for Dan. Kathy's top priority in life was the happiness of her husband and children. She had no personal interest in visiting Disney World, but knew that it would make her family happy. Religion was important but only served as part of an infrastructure that supported her devotion to her family. She loved a good time as much as the next woman — enjoyed big parties, dining out, moderate consumption of alcohol, and yes, a healthy amount of sex. But all of these served only to sustain her primary functions — being a good wife and mother. On top of that, she was an avid reader, an excellent cook, and a reasonable tennis player. Dan realized that he married a wonderful, albeit complex, woman. He realized it more now than when they were first married.

Kathy was waiting for Dan's response about Sunday Mass, anticipating another little argument about Catholic rules. Instead, she found him staring blankly at the Cheshire reptile. They were both a bit weary after trekking through Universal Studios, then spending two hours at the pool in the afternoon sun. She sipped on her perfect Manhattan and savored it, pleasantly surprised to find that the Dolphin bartender understood the exact mix of sweet and dry vermouths required to make a Manhattan-on-the-rocks a "perfect" Manhattan. She enjoyed her time alone with Dan. It was a rarity at home, save for their occasional nights out for dinner. Being alone while traveling was somehow even more satisfying — a change in venue always seemed to allow time for healthy introspection.

She knew that Dan arranged this vacation mostly for the kids, but she loved him for doing that. He really was a good father, even if his work prevented him from spending a lot of time with the kids at home. She never once heard any of her children complain about their dad's absence. When he missed Mass on Sundays because he was rounding at the hospital, Kathy would explain to their children that "your father is doing God's work." And she really believed that he was. She realized that fifteen years earlier, she succeeded in steering Dan back to Ohio. He could have trained at Columbia, Cornell, Yale, or one of the Harvard hospitals, but he followed her back to their hometown. She would spend the rest of her life trying to make him happy that he made that decision. Differences of opinions about things like their religious beliefs would not stand in her way.

"Well, except for the so-called reptiles and dolphins, this has been a wonderful little vacation, Dan."

"Yeah, let's make it an annual tradition," Dan responded. "Are you ready for another round of drinks?"

Eight

Hong Kong and China —
October 1993

Standing at the top of a long segment of the Great Wall of China opened to tourists, with icy rain falling and making for a slick ascent, Dan looked down sweating and breathing rapidly — and got a special feeling. The whole experience was a bit touristy — cheap souvenirs being sold at the base of the climb and at several locations along the way to the top. But climbing the wall was not for the weak or faint-of-heart; it was an athletic feat and a special moment. The "stairs" of the Great Wall were built unevenly — sometimes almost two feet tall, and in other sections so flat that it was almost like ascending a slick ramp. A number of climbers settled for ascending only part-way up before turning back to the base.

"How many times in our lives will we get to do this? We're going to the top, baby." It was Kathy speaking, not Dan. But as they approached the "summit" of this section of the Wall, Kathy was a few steps behind Dan. He wanted to be the winner. When she reached the top a few moments later, they held each other and stared into the misty Chinese countryside below, each separately thinking about ancient civilizations, wars, and a totally different culture on the opposite side of the planet. Dan remembered the song "Do you feel like I do?"

The trip to China started out badly. Continental Airlines had no direct flights to Hong Kong, so from Cleveland there were stops and long layovers in Los Angeles, Honolulu, and Guam. Including the layovers, the trip took more than twenty-four hours and most of the flights occurred in the dark of night. Flying business-first class all the way made the long journey palatable as there were frequent meals and an endless supply of booze or wine. As they crossed the International Date Line, Dan tried to remember Einstein's theory of relativity to decide if he was now fifteen seconds older or fifteen seconds younger than he was at the start of the trip.

They landed in Hong Kong, spent forty-five minutes in the long line for passport clearance, and then waited for more than thirty minutes at baggage claim until it was clear that their baggage had not arrived. The twenty-four hour trip was now up to twenty-six hours. Apparently their bags were lost in Guam. Unfortunately, Continental only flew to Hong Kong through Guam three times a week, so it would take at least two to three days for the airline to deliver the luggage. They had no idea what forwarding address to leave with the baggage office because their complicated itinerary called for trips to several cities in a short period of time. The best they could do was to hand the baggage officer the business card of their host in Hong Kong — Peter Yang from Sandoz China.

Dan and Kathy were scheduled to meet Mr. Yang in Hong Kong, have dinner, and fly to Wuhan the next morning. Each of them was wearing running clothes — sweatpants and sweatshirts

— for the long flight. After realizing that their luggage was lost for at least two days, they taxied into downtown Hong Kong and met Peter and one his colleagues at the Conrad Hotel, immediately apologizing for their state of undress. Their hosts were more than gracious and suggested a visit to *Marks and Spencer* immediately after dinner, paying — in cash — for Dan's purchase of two new suits, four new shirts, a pair of shoes, ties and underwear, and for whatever Kathy needed for at least the next few days. *Maybe a thousand British pounds in up-front cash? They'd never get away with this in the United States — a direct payoff to a physician and a major conflict of interest.* Their hosts assured them that they would track down the luggage, but Dan and Kathy weren't quite sure when or in what Chinese city they would come across their clothes and other belongings.

Dan easily found a couple of beautiful suits — probably the nicest he had ever purchased. High quality and quickly tailored suits were one of Hong Kong's claims to fame, but luckily, Dan was able to find some well-fitting suits right off the rack. Kathy's situation was more problematic. She quietly selected some needed underwear, but at 5 feet 8 inches, she appeared like the Fifty Foot Woman to the Chinese citizens of Hong Kong and it was virtually impossible to find a dress, skirt or pantsuit that fit. And there was no time for a fitting and later tailoring. It was getting late and their Chinese hosts suggested that she wait to buy clothes in the mainland.

By Chinese standards, Wuhan was a small city (only nine million people) located in the east-central portion of the country, at the intersection of the Han and Yangtze Rivers. The airport was small and Dan was sure that it had not been renovated — or even repainted — since the revolution of 1949. The entire building was a concoction of military-style green walls with peeling paint. The drive from the airport to the hotel was dominated by images of bicycles and peasants carrying bags of food, bricks of coal, and other goods on rickshaws. The air was thickly filled with the odor of burning coal, which was the major fuel used for heating Chinese homes and buildings.

The main reason for visiting Wuhan was a trip to Tongji Medical University — the busiest transplant program in China. Chinese culture did not accept the concept of brain death, so all transplants were performed using living donors. It was widely rumored that executed prisoners were the main source for "living" donors, but this topic was absolutely off-limits on this trip. Most of the transplants performed in China were kidney or liver transplants, but Dan had become an international expert on cyclosporine, and his role in China was to visit with transplant physicians and surgeons from major transplant centers in several cities to teach them about the revolutionary drug that was only rarely used in China at the time. He was an expert in the field of heart transplantation, but for these talks in China he mostly focused on experiences with cyclosporine in kidney transplantation. Most Chinese transplant recipients were treated with a variety of herbs believed to have immunosuppressive properties. Amazingly, one-year graft survival rates were comparable to those being reported in the United States.

Cyclosporine, a natural product of a mold discovered growing in a northern European swamp *(Yummy!)*, was originally isolated as a drug capable of killing parasites. Further research showed that the drug potently inhibited the activation of T-lymphocytes, the white blood cells responsible for rejection of transplanted organs. The use of cyclosporine revolutionized the field of kidney transplantation, vastly improving short-term outcomes. Within a few years of its introduction in the early 1980s, transplantation of kidneys — historically the first organs transplanted — became substantially more successful, and the number of transplant centers grew rapidly around the world. In addition, transplantation of organs other than the kidney — liver, heart, lung, and pancreas — became a reality.

While Dan initially scoffed at the idea of preventing allograft rejection with herbs, he ultimately realized that there was no reason to believe that the natural products of those herbs were any less likely to inhibit T-cells than the product of a European swamp mold. He found the Chinese doctors to be skeptical about Western drugs but always gracious and anxious to learn. In return, he was surprised that he learned as much from the Chinese transplant physicians and surgeons as they did from his lectures.

A pleasant hostess accompanied Dan and Kathy to Wuhan's best department store so Kathy could buy some clothes. It seemed more like a military outlet store than a department store. Buying clothes for Kathy in Wuhan was NOT a good idea. Most citizens of this interior city had never seen Westerners — let alone a Fifty Foot Woman. It was impossible for Kathy to walk through the store without hordes of Chinese women walking up to stroke her arms and legs. *Maybe I'll zap these small oriental creatures with my laser-emitting eyeballs!* She felt uncomfortable shopping for clothes and would have to wait until they arrived in Beijing two days later. Her sweat suit was getting ripe, but at least she had clean underwear.

The general scheme was for Dan to give one or two talks each morning followed by carefully planned excursions to Chinese tourist attractions each afternoon. Dan had prepared a set of Kodachrome slides that would normally fill a fifty minute presentation at any U.S. center. After his first talk in Wuhan, he quickly realized that he would have to dramatically reduce the number of slides. Interestingly, virtually all of the transplant surgeons in China had trained in the United States or in Europe and spoke at least some English. However, the local tradition was to use a Chinese interpreter for talks by American speakers. This meant that Dan would literally pause after each slide to allow the interpreter to translate his comments. He was perplexed that some of his longest and scientifically most complex remarks were often distilled to just a few syllables, while some of his simplest comments prompted long orations in Chinese, often accompanied by bodily gyrations. *What the heck? What did I say?* Occasionally these interpretations would elicit unexpected chuckles from the audience when he had said nothing particularly funny and on more than one occasion, Dan wondered whether his brilliant descriptions of results from clinical trials with cyclosporine were being translated into Chinese jokes. By the end of his tour, he had reduced his slides from sixty to thirty, but everyone, including the ever-present representatives from Sandoz, appeared to be satisfied with his presentations.

Sandoz had arranged for English-speaking guides to accompany Kathy and Dan everywhere they went. Frankly, the language barrier was so intense outside of hotels that they couldn't imagine how they would have survived the visit to China without these helpers. While Dan gave his talks, the guides were instructed to take Kathy on shopping sprees. Kathy loved interacting with the guides — most often young men or women in their twenties. She had less interest in natural or architectural landmarks than she did in hearing about their personal lives. *Where were you born? How many brothers and sisters do you have? What do your parents do? How long did you go to school? When did you learn to speak English? Are you married? Have a girlfriend or boyfriend? Have you ever been to Cleveland?* It seemed that the guides were delighted to participate in these exchanges — it gave them a chance to practice their English, but also to learn more about strangers from the western hemisphere.

Sometimes, the guides were more like bodyguards. In 1993, China had two currencies — one for citizens and one for foreigners. Illegal trade for the cheaper local currency was a major criminal activity in the big cities, and Dan and Kathy witnessed a number of western visitors being accosted by money traders. The guides were well-trained to recognize these criminals and also were adept at using a few choice Chinese comments to scare them off. Taxi cab rip-offs of western travelers were also common. Because the guides were provided with plenty of cash to show their guests a good time, Dan and Kathy never had to worry about paying their own money for taxis, admission fees to tourist attractions, food, or anything else. They were being treated like royalty in a land of peasants.

For two weeks, Dan and Kathy felt like rock stars on a coast-to-coast tour, staying in no single Chinese city for more than two days, with a three-day stay in Beijing being the only exception. When they arrived at the Great China Hotel in Beijing, they were greeted at the front desk with a message that their luggage had been found. While Kathy checked into the room, Dan was escorted by his guide back to the international airport where he was frisked three times. All of the luggage was opened and the contents spilled out on the floor of a large garage space for examination. China was in the process of westernization but this little ordeal seemed very foreign and military-like. *No problem at all — at least we have our clothes.*

The Great China Hotel was more opulent than any hotel Dan or Kathy had ever seen in the United States or Europe. The place was westernized on a grand scale.

This was Dan's "star" system for hotels: white robes — two stars; robes and a bathroom scale — three stars; robes, scale, separate bathtub and shower — four stars; all of the above and a mini-bar — five stars. With all of these elements *plus* a large Jacuzzi in a bathroom that was as big as their entire bedroom at home, the Great China Hotel was off the scoring chart. But when they left their hotel for a short walk on their first night in Beijing, they were horrified to find people living in cardboard or tin huts on the streets in the adjacent neighborhood. It was late fall, the weather was cool and damp, and the smell of burning coal was everywhere, stinging the eyes. Old women were cleaning the streets of the city with long brooms — like those of witches. Witnessing the stark contrast between opulence and poverty, Dan could only think out loud, "I wish our children could be here for just an hour to see what we are seeing."

Each night ended with a Chinese feast at a top restaurant in the host city. Dan and Kathy were joined by the local Sandoz representatives and by the local transplant physicians and surgeons. Generally, the feast was served at a round table large enough for twelve to sixteen people. There were multiple servings of food, all shared "Chinese style" with each dinner guest sharing the same platter of food. The seating arrangements were of utmost importance to the Chinese attendees, with the most important local doctors sitting closest to the guests. For a table of sixteen people, it usually took twenty to thirty minutes to establish the appropriate seating hierarchy.

It was difficult for Dan and Kathy to recognize many of the local dishes, but the Sandoz representatives were very helpful, broadly categorizing each plate as "meat," "fish," or "fowl." Beverages almost always were limited to tea and warm beer — no water, no Diet Coke, and certainly no manhattans or martinis. With each set of reps, Kathy and Dan established some pre-dinner guidelines: absolutely no cat or dog meat. They forgot about snake, which they ended up eating on several occasions, only to be told after the fact. *Not bad at all, tasted like chicken.* They recognized and avoided eel — a banquet favorite for the Chinese, but too close to resembling a giant slug or a large ball of snot as far as they were concerned. On their last night in Beijing, the Sandoz reps announced a surprise: a special visit to a restaurant serving western food! They sampled cheeseburgers, breaded pork chops, hot dogs, and a few other "American" classics that were prepared in a not-so-tasty manner *(maybe it was dog meat?)*. It was their only bad meal during the entire trip.

That night, Kathy commented about how gracious all the Chinese doctors had been on this trip. "I could hardly tell the difference between the medical doctors and the surgeons."

"You mean you can tell that difference in the United States?"

"Oh, definitely. In the United States, most surgeons have an aura of aggressiveness, assertiveness, and confidence. Most internists are passive, even submissive."

"How incredibly simplistic! Are you including *me* in those generalizations?"

"Sure I am, but I still love ya, hon," she said with a hint of sarcasm, giving Dan a gentle kiss on the cheek.

Dan was intrigued by Kathy's perception. He never thought of himself as passive, but he, too, had recognized a difference in medical and surgical personalities throughout his career — fully cognizant that he himself was a frustrated surgeon. He often wished he had gone with his own instincts in medical school and chosen surgery over medicine. *Fixing someone's illness with your own hands – not just by signing prescriptions for drugs.* Some of his colleagues in internal medicine looked down on surgeons as mere technicians. Conversely, many surgeons looked down on internists as ethereal eggheads. These concepts rarely, if ever, were discussed openly because, at the end of the day, surgeons needed internists to fuel their business, and internists needed surgeons to manage many disease states. But there were always subtle tensions.

In the field of organ transplantation, there was an absolute need for internists to work with surgeons. This interdisciplinary approach was best for the care of patients — at least when things were going well. When something went wrong with a patient, it was easy to start pointing fingers. From Dan's point of view, he benefited from being a frustrated surgeon who was paired with Jack Hurtuk, a frustrated internist. Jack had basic training in transplant immunology that far exceeded Dan's. Dan always took an interest in surgical details, while Jack liked to help with medical management. They complemented each other in a unique way — undoubtedly accounting for much of the success of the CMC transplant program.

Thinking about life back in Cleveland made Dan realize that they were nearing the half-way point of this visit to China. After whirlwind trips through Shanghai *(very European)* and Guangzhou *(reminds me of L.A.)*, more lavish banquets, a boating and fishing excursion on the River Li in southern China (the area famous for the tall, peaked mountains that adorn the backgrounds of old Chinese prints), they returned home. On the long flight home from Hong Kong, they reviewed all of the exotic stories that they would share with their young children. The trip would forever change their perspective on the American way of life. It solidified Dan's notion that travel was essential to comprehending his own life.

On the long journey home, Kathy recounted all the elements of their trip and said repeatedly, "We are so lucky."

Nine

December 19, 1994

There were warning signs for at least two months. *Master clinician and I didn't realize that my own son was seriously sick.* Michael had been playing peewee hockey for three years, just like his brother Tom before him. Twice in November, the coach sent Michael home from practice early when he complained of chest pains. *A cardiologist and I can't recognize the cause of chest pain in an eleven-year-old boy.* "You think he's acting out?" Dan asked Kathy incredulously. "He's been such a good athlete. Maybe he can't stand the competition at this level."

Dan and Kathy had established a family Christmas tradition of taking a day off work during the weeks before the holiday and bringing the kids to Tower City, the shopping mall that was part of downtown's Terminal Tower complex. The twins were still willing to visit Santa for probably the last year, and

Tom and Michael went along happily for the food and shopping. The older boys also were now big enough to enjoy the *Elf Shop* where they were able to buy their parents Christmas gifts for less than five bucks — using their parents' money of course. Dan would inevitably get a new pair of socks and Kathy a new Christmas tree ornament — but it was the thought that counted. Kathy loved Christmas and loved teaching her kids about the spirit of giving and receiving. They topped off the afternoon with pizza and sodas from *Mama's Pizza Shop*. In the late afternoon walk back to the Tower City parking lot, Michael stopped twice, complaining that he was short of breath. For the first time, Dan recognized that Michael looked pale.

"Kathy, I think Michael may be anemic," Dan told Kathy later that night. Kathy seemed less concerned but agreed to make an appointment with the pediatrician before Christmas.

December 19 would forever be considered Black Monday for the Ulek family.

During Dan's afternoon clinic, the secretary interrupted him with an urgent call from Jim Wassenstein — Michael's pediatrician. "Hi Dan, I ran a complete blood count on Michael and you were right — he's quite anemic. Hematocrit is 19 percent. But Dan, his platelets are also low at 11,000. Kathy tells me he's had no bleeding. Dan, there are some abnormal cells — I want you to get him down to Children's CMC and see Susan Sampson as soon as possible."

"Okay. Susan Sampson from Peds Oncology?" asked Dan.

"Yes. Dan this could be — not sure — it could be — leukemia. The abnormal cells are blasts."

"Jesus — when should we see Susan?"

"Today, Dan — I'll get Michael in to see Sampson this afternoon."

It was 1:30 p.m. Dan had eight more patients scheduled and quickly told the clinic staff he had a family emergency that would require cancelling the rest of his patients. There were no arguments from the staff, which could tell from his strained facial expression that something was seriously wrong.

He called Kathy while driving home. "Hi hon. Did Wassenstein call you?" He suddenly realized that he didn't know whether Kathy had been apprised of the lab results or of the differential diagnosis.

"No, why?"

"I'm on my way home. Wassenstein is arranging an appointment for Michael to see a hematologist at Children's CMC this afternoon."

"This afternoon? It's almost two o'clock. And we have the department Christmas cocktail party tonight."

"We'll need to cancel."

He could tell by the silent pause on the phone that he had just scared Kathy. He was scared, too. Thinking back to his residency years, he once thought of going into Hematology-Oncology, but was dissuaded by his experience caring for patients with leukemia. Not only were the patients sick as hell, they were probably the most labor intensive patients from a resident's perspective. Both before and after chemotherapy, they required multiple transfusions — red blood cells, platelets, plasma. Because their white blood cell counts were low, every fever spike prompted multiple cultures and gram stains — of blood, urine, and other body fluids — looking for signs of infection. A simple headache would mandate a spinal tap to rule out meningitis. Every cough prompted a chest x-ray. The typical patient was in the hospital for weeks and required so many intravenous lines and blood draws that they often ran out of visible veins. In those days, central venous catheters were not used commonly and care of these patients depended on access to peripheral veins on the arms or legs, sometimes even on the torso or scalp. Dan recalled spending hours attempting to find venous access on a single patient, repeatedly apologizing for the painful needle sticks. Because the platelet counts also were low, the patients were at risk for spontaneous bleeding — and every needle stick resulted in a bloody mess — so these vein-finding sessions often ended in a blood bath. Cleaning up the mess could itself take an hour.

The patients were miserable and suffered terribly from the side effects of chemotherapy. But most importantly — they almost always died. Oh, there were short-term remissions, but relapses were the rule, and few patients lived for more than six months. The relapses were more resistant to treatment and so even more powerful and more toxic chemotherapeutic drugs were used in what Dan felt was a futile effort, only making the patients sicker before their inevitable deaths. *If I ever developed this disease, I would refuse all treatment, take care of my affairs, buy a case of Glenlivet, and try to enjoy the remaining few months of my life.*

But those patients that he cared for during residency were adults who most often had acute *myelogenous* leukemia (AML). As a child, Michael was statistically more likely to have acute *lymphocytic* leukemia (ALL). Although Dan had not kept up with the Heme-Onc literature, he remembered that the prognosis of ALL was considerably better than AML, and that a substantial number of children could be cured. Moreover, chemotherapies had improved since his training years, and bone marrow transplantation — once extremely experimental — was now performed routinely for patients with acute leukemia with outcomes that were increasingly successful. And maybe Wassenstein was wrong — maybe Michael has something other than leukemia. *I'll be optimistic as hell when I explain all this to Kathy.*

When he arrived home, Dan found Michael asleep on the family room couch — a familiar sight for the past few weeks, only now making sense. *His hematocrit is 19 percent! How could I miss that?* Apparently Kathy decided to keep Michael home from school after the visit with Wassenstein — beginning his Christmas vacation a day early. The other kids would be coming home to begin their Christmas break in a couple of hours.

He found Kathy upstairs changing clothes for the trip downtown to the CMC. If she was scared, it sure didn't show. She looked remarkably calm and collected. But then Kathy was always the optimist in their relationship. She often criticized Dan for being the opposite. *Okay, Mr. Doom and Gloom.* He was always worried about money, the kids' educations, whether everything he had achieved could somehow collapse some day. Even in his professional life, nurses or other colleagues would sometimes pull him aside after a patient interaction, noting that maybe he could have emphasized more the potential *positive* outcomes than the *negative* ones when discussing treatment options and prognoses. *Dr. Doom and Gloom.*

"So is this anemia so critical to warrant a late afternoon visit before the holiday?" asked Kathy.

"Hon, Wassenstein is worried about more than just anemia. Michael's red blood cell count or hematocrit is 19 percent when normal is closer to 40 percent. His blood smear shows blasts. Those are immature white blood cells that are usually found only in the bone marrow and almost never in normal blood. And his other counts are low. There's the possibility of something more serious than anemia — maybe leukemia." *I had intended to be optimistic. That didn't come out right — in fact my voice was quivering.*

"Dan, you look worried. Do you really think it's something serious?"

"I don't know Kath, but one way or another I feel terrible about missing Michael's signs and symptoms. As I think of it, seems like he's been sleeping excessively since late summer. If it's just anemia, it's probably been going on for four months and I never caught on."

Kathy called Dan's mom and asked if she could drive over to take care of the other kids for a few hours when they got home from school. "Michael has anemia and Dan and I are taking him down to CMC — probably needs a prescription for iron. We should be back by five."

They were not back by five. The next twenty-four hours were like a family trip to hell.

Sue Sampson was an attractive pediatric oncologist with a national reputation for her work with bone cancers and other childhood malignancies. Dan figured she was about his age, tall, dark skin, thick brunette hair *(maybe Italian or Greek? He presumed that Sampson was her married name, based on the sizeable diamond on her ring finger).* Their paths rarely crossed academically, although he spent a year with her on the medical school's Promotion and Tenure Committee and found her to be not just attractive, but smart and logical, with strong opinions that often swayed the committee. He also knew there were rumors that she was the heir apparent to the Department Chair in Pediatrics.

Dan had anticipated that Sue would first meet with him and Kathy before examining Michael, but instead she met with all three. Michael was seated between his parents in a small conference room. Sue Sampson did not dress like the typical pediatrician — no playful clothes or little fuzzy bunnies attached to her stethoscope. At this and all future meetings she would wear a knee-length dress — mostly covered by her immaculately clean white lab coat — appearing very professional. In all of their subsequent encounters, Dan never saw her wear the same dress twice.

"Michael, I'm Dr. Sampson. Did Dr. Wassenstein or your parents tell you why you are here?"

"Anemia. I get tired," said Michael, providing an honest assessment of what he had assimilated thus far.

"We asked Dr. Wassenstein to Bonnie Speed your blood samples from this morning to our laboratory. I've reviewed the blood smears and it appears that you have leukemia."

Dan's faint hope for some other diagnosis flew out the window. He had some sudden flashbacks to his days as a resident on the Heme-Onc ward at OSU and was struggling to pay attention to Sue Sampson.

She went on. "Do you know what leukemia is, Michael?"

"Mom, is that what Katie Richert had?"

Kathy glanced at Dan knowingly as it just dawned on both of them that their neighbors, Jim and Louise Richert, had a daughter who died of leukemia at the age of five — long before the Uleks moved into the neighborhood. The other Richert kids were good friends of the Ulek kids and often talked about their sister Katie.

With surprisingly little facial expression, Michael looked directly at Sue Sampson and asked, "Am I going to die?"

Dan feigned a cough and turned away from his son to conceal his welling tears. It was rare that his adult patients asked that kind of question so directly. Hearing it from his eleven-year-old son was painfully unexpected and took his breath away. But it turned out to be the first and *last* time that Dan ever heard Michael speak about his illness with any sense of negativity.

Sampson was clearly experienced with these kinds of encounters. "Yes, Michael, you might die from leukemia, but we now have good treatments, and we are going to do everything we can to prevent that from happening. You and your parents will be very busy in the next week and we need to start treatment right away."

"Busy?" asked Michael, thinking about Christmas this coming Sunday.

"We need to admit you to the hospital today. You will need minor surgery tonight for a bone marrow test and the placement of two special IV lines that we'll use for the treatment." She nodded to Dan. "Broviac catheters for blood draws, transfusions, and chemo."

"My nurse will come in to tell you more about the bone marrow test while I step outside to talk to your mom and dad. We're going to get you well, Michael." Kathy had been shaken briefly by the unexpected announcement of a hospital admission, but she loved Sampson's direct and optimistic style.

In the hallway, she gave Dan and Kathy a more detailed plan. Michael would need a bone marrow biopsy immediately in order to characterize the type of leukemia. "Hard to tell by the peripheral blood smear alone, but it's probably acute lymphocytic leukemia in this age group. Do you have other children?"

"Three," Kathy replied. "All home now starting their Christmas vacation. Why do you ask?"

"We'll need them all here tomorrow morning for HLA typing — tissue typing. These days, the best outcomes occur with bone marrow transplants. We first give chemotherapy — the type depends on the type of leukemia — to eradicate the leukemic bone marrow. Depending on the type of leukemia, we generally administer two separate rounds of chemotherapy to assure complete eradication of the leukemia. Then, if and when we obtain a remission with no signs of residual leukemic cells, we perform a bone marrow transplant, hopefully replacing the recipient's sick marrow with a new healthy marrow from the donor. But the donor pretty much needs to be HLA identical — a perfect match. So keep your fingers crossed that one of your other three children matches Michael."

"If not?" asked Kathy.

"Well, we'll ask for you and Dan to get tissue typed, too, but it is almost impossible for a parent to be a perfect match to one of their own children. If none of the family members match, we would have to put Michael on the waiting list for a non-family donor — and unfortunately that can be a very long wait. Some children with leukemia can achieve long remissions or even cures with chemotherapy alone, but the best outcomes are achieved with a subsequent bone marrow transplant, so that's the goal."

Susan went on. "We are going to proceed with the bone marrow biopsy shortly. My nurse is in the examining room and will need to start an IV for ketamine anesthesia — puts Michael in la-la land for about fifteen minutes. The biopsy is a quick procedure — I'll simply aspirate a tube of marrow from his iliac crest." For Kathy's sake, she pointed to her own backside to indicate the bony iliac crest in the lower back, forming the back end of the hip joint. "Then we'll admit him — probably to Children's Four — and I've already made arrangements with General Surgery for placement of the Broviacs later tonight. Nothing will start in earnest until we see the bone marrow results tomorrow. Unless you have any other questions, my advice is for the three of us to go back in the room and tell Michael the plan. One or both of you is more than welcome to stay with him tonight or any night while he's here — all the rooms in Children's are equipped with sleeping cots for parents — but I strongly suggest that you go home tonight and talk to your other children. Last thing — the chemotherapy is tough. He'll almost certainly need blood and platelet transfusions. His white blood cell count will fall and put him at risk for infection so he will likely need antibiotics. The two rounds of chemotherapy will actually take place over a few months and Michael may need to be in the hospital more than once if he develops any signs of infection. And only if we achieve leukemic remission do we proceed with the transplant. I'm afraid this might not be the merriest of Christmas holidays for you guys."

Kathy was very impressed with Dr. Sampson's direct yet sympathetic style. It was obvious that she had been through this professional routine many times before, but she could still comfortably explain things from a layperson's and a mother's perspective.

"I want to come back and stay with Michael tonight," said Kathy. "I need to be with him tonight."

Ten

December 20, 1994

Dan was trying to recollect if any of the kids ever had even a simple blood test, let alone being phlebotomized for the ten tubes of blood required from each member of the family for tissue typing. But even the twins, Lauren and Brian — now eight years old — handled the procedure stoically, barely wincing from the needle sticks. They didn't quite understand everything that Mom and Dad had tried to explain the night before, but they knew that their brother Michael was "very, very" sick and that somehow they were helping him to get better.

Dan was of course very familiar with tissue typing because it was relevant to both bone marrow and solid organ transplantation. Every person has six transplant tissue types, also known as human leukocyte antigens or HLA antigens. Any two people could match one another on a scale of 0 to 6 antigen matches with

6 matches being "perfect." Children inherit three HLA antigens from each parent. So, depending on whether the sibling inherited the same chromosomes from mother and father, the statistical possibilities of matching among siblings are: 25 percent chance of a 0 out of 6 match, 50 percent chance of a 3 out of 6 match, and 25 percent chance of a 6 out of 6 match. Here's where bone marrow transplantation differs from heart and other solid organ transplants like kidneys or livers. The latter can be performed successfully even when the tissue matching is minimal. For a bone marrow transplant, a perfect match is almost essential for success. Even minor mismatching (for example, 1 out of 6 mismatched HLA antigens) would increase the chances of a dreaded and sometimes fatal complication called graft versus host disease (GVHD) in which white blood cells from the transplanted donor marrow attack the tissues and organs of the recipient.

Dan had explained all this to Kathy the night before. After he took the last turn with the ten-tube blood draw, he looked up from his reclining chair and winked at his wife. "Feeling lucky?" He felt like he was participating in a crap shoot.

"I prayed last night, Dan. We *will* have a perfect match." For ever more, prayer would become a part of Kathy's daily routine.

After the tissue typing, the entire family went to visit Michael in his hospital room in Children's Hospital.

"Wow, this place is cool," Lauren beamed. "You don't look sick, Michael."

"I'm gonna be fine. Hey, look in that cupboard — I got tons of videogames and my own computer and TV. I got Dr. Sampson and she's great. Look at these tubes in my chest — I didn't feel anything — woke up and these Broviacs were here."

Lauren and Brian suspiciously examined the catheters poking out of the upper portion of Michael's chest under a small bandage, feeling some combination of nausea and awe.

Dan thought that Michael's attitude and demeanor were remarkable. Maybe he didn't quite understand the seriousness of his illness. But in fact, it seemed that he *did* understand, and that he was doing everything possible to calm his brothers and sister — and his parents as well. Most patients with newly diagnosed malignancies go through classic phases of anger and denial before ultimately accepting their fate. Maybe it was Michael's young age, maybe Michael was just a unique human being but it seemed that he had quickly reached a level of understanding and acceptance. Dan was intrigued and puzzled, and would ponder the phenomenon for years to come.

Kathy drove Tom, Lauren and Brian home and planned to come back later to stay with Michael overnight once again. *Thank God for Dan's mom. We are going to need her babysitting services more than ever the next few weeks.* Dan stayed in Michael's room making phone calls to arrange for urgent coverage of his clinics when Sue Sampson walked in. Michael was sound asleep. "I was hoping Kathy would still be here. I have great news — Lauren is a perfect match."

"She prayed."

"I'm sorry?"

"Nothing Sue. That *is* great news. So now that it's just you and me, tell me what you think about the prognosis."

Sue motioned for him to move out to the hallway. "I gave you the good news, Dan. The bad news is that Michael has AML, not ALL. It's rare in children but the tests are definitive."

"Oh my God. Do kids with AML do better than adults?"

"The prognosis is worse than with ALL — substantially worse. The best bet is a bone marrow transplant so the news about Lauren is good. With a successful transplant, five-year survival rates are up to 30 percent."

Dan pretended to be uplifted but, in fact, was devastated. A five-year survival rate of 30 percent is not what he considered to be good news for an eleven-year-old boy. He wanted to pick up the phone immediately and call Kathy but decided to wait till she returned to the hospital later that evening. In the mean time, he made several calls to his staff and colleagues to provide updates. He called Jack Hurtuk in his office between cases in the operating room.

"Dan, I am sorry to hear about your son. Sue Sampson is great, though. What does she have to say?" Jack asked.

"Thirty percent five-year survival, Jack. Thirty percent five-year survival. Michael is as good as dead."

"Listen, you should consider taking your son to Sloan Kettering, MD Anderson in Houston, the University of Washington, or maybe Hopkins. CMC has a great track record in general pediatric oncology, but those places are the real centers of excellence when it comes to bone marrow transplantation. By the way, don't worry about the service. We've been talking all day and coverage will not be a problem. You take as much time as you need to get your son healthy. And Dan, think seriously about going to one of the big leukemia centers."

What Jack didn't understand was the pressure that Dan was under to increase his revenues from clinical activities. A month earlier, he had a meeting with Rick Weichel. In contrast to many of his colleagues who performed lucrative procedures such as cardiac catheterizations, placement of pacemakers and other electrophysiological procedures, Dan had opted for a career in "noninvasive" cardiology as a basis for his current work in heart transplantation. Even the surveillance heart transplant biopsies — performed on transplant recipients almost monthly during the first year after the transplant using a procedure akin to a standard cardiac catheterization — were performed by one of Dan's colleagues who specialized in "invasive" procedures. Unfortunately, insurance companies rewarded procedural skills more robustly than they did cognitive skills. Department chairs tried to compensate for this by creating relative value units or RVUs, based on some relative value of every patient encounter. But in Dan's mind, RVUs were still heavily weighted toward procedures and he felt that the system was unfair. While the invasive cardiologist spent less than an hour doing a surveillance biopsy, Dan might spend three hours reviewing the biopsy with a pathologist, discussing the results with the staff, the patient and the family, and making treatment decisions. But his RVUs for these efforts were less than a quarter of what his colleagues earned for performing the procedure.

Weichel met with Dan to review his RVUs for the past six months. Weichel was a tall man, maybe 6 feet 5 inches, with an athletic frame and angular facial features — very imposing in either social or professional encounters. "You're running below the seventieth percentile of the Division's benchmark based on national standards for academic cardiology. I'm happy to hear that your NIH grant was renewed recently, but it only provides a 20 percent effort toward your salary support. If you can't get your RVUs closer to the eightieth percentile, I am going to have a hard time justifying your salary during the spring budget meetings with the Department of Medicine.

Weichel leaned closer and peered into Dan's eyes, "You might consider cutting down on travel."

Dan had been waiting for this. He was considered a rising star in the academic world and had been invited to join speaker bureaus sponsored by several of the pharmaceutical companies that produced immunosuppressive drugs used for transplant recipients. His research focused on the development of simple urine tests that measured metabolic products of molecules involved in immune rejection of a transplanted organ — molecules that were ultimately excreted by the kidneys into the urine. These novel tests could theoretically help transplant physicians in adjusting the doses of immunosuppressive drugs, and thus were of great interest to the pharmaceutical industry. During the past year, Dan had traveled two to four times each month to give invited talks sponsored by educational grants from the drug companies. Each of his talks, whether in the United States or abroad, provided an honorarium ranging from $1,000 to $2,500 apiece — a substantial little perk, especially for someone earning the salary of an academic physician. The current policy in the Department of Medicine at CMC allowed faculty members to retain such honoraria. This sort of outside income was only a source of friction when the travel required an inordinate amount of coverage by fellow faculty members, or when it adversely affected other sources of revenue such as grants or clinical income from patient care — the revenues that supported one's base salary.

"What about bringing prestige to the institution? Just last year you told me that both national and international recognition would be critical when it comes time for promotion to full professor of medicine," Dan protested.

"It's a delicate balance Dan. And frankly, academic promotion has nothing to do with balancing my divisional budget."

The timing of Michael's illness couldn't have been worse. Seeking care at a world-renowned leukemia center in another part of the country might require weeks or months of time away when Dan could not afford to miss even a few days worth of RVUs. Besides, he and Kathy were very impressed with Sue Sampson. Dan decided quickly — with Kathy's blessing — that, to the extent possible, he would not miss any work because of Michael's leukemia. He also called two local pharmaceutical representatives and cancelled three west coast talks that had been scheduled for January.

Kathy returned to the hospital around 6:00 p.m. and the nursing staff allowed Michael to go the cafeteria with his parents for a dinner of hot dogs and French fries. Michael received transfusions of three units of packed red blood cells earlier in the day and was feeling great — more energetic than he had felt in months. The chemotherapy was going to begin in the morning and Dan knew that his son's appetite might not be good for some time, so he encouraged Michael to finish up all of his fries.

Toward the end of their meal, Dan decided to pop the good news. "Guess what? Dr. Sampson talked to me earlier about our tissue typing and told me that Lauren is a perfect match. A six out of six match. That means she can donate her bone marrow to cure your leukemia!"

Kathy closed her eyes tightly, clearly responding to the God who had answered her prayers. When they returned to Michael's hospital room, Dan told his son that he needed to talk with Mom about things at home. He escorted Kathy to an empty consultation room.

"Listen, I didn't have the heart to tell Michael that he has AML, not ALL — he really wouldn't understand anyway — but that's the other news that Sampson delivered today. What an emotional roller coaster."

"Dan, I don't understand either."

"Acute *myelogenous* leukemia is uncommon in kids." He got up to close the door. "The treatment is awful and the prognosis is horrible." He started sobbing. "Kathy, Michael is going to die." He remembered crying at his father's funeral but was not sure if Kathy had ever seen him sobbing as uncontrollably as he was now.

After a long pause, Kathy chimed in. "Listen Mr. Doom and Gloom, I don't believe anything you are saying. God answered my prayer and gave us a daughter who is a perfect match. He will answer all my prayers and he will cure Michael. He will, Dan — I know it. I will not give in to your pessimism. Are you with me or not?"

"Kathy, when I was a resident taking care of patients with AML, I always told myself that if I ever contracted the disease, I would never put myself through the torture of treatment — I would just walk away, perhaps a long, long way, and die peacefully. I had hoped that treatments had improved over the years, but Sue Sampson tells me the prognosis for AML is not much better than it was twenty years ago. The five-year survival rate is only 30 percent."

He looked up to find Kathy looking determined and unfazed. She stood up and said nothing further.

"All right, I won't impose my own feelings on Michael — or on you. Michael is eleven years old. He will never see me crying like this. I am with you, hon, but I am really afraid."

Eleven

A Winter of Discontent — 1994 to 1995

Michael tolerated his first round of chemotherapy reasonably well, thanks to ondansetron — at that time a relatively new anti-emetic drug that was very effective in reducing nausea and vomiting associated with chemotherapy. In fact, Sue Sampson reluctantly agreed to give Michael a pass to come home on Christmas Eve, with the understanding that he would return to the hospital by early afternoon on Christmas Day. The family tradition was to open gifts on Christmas morning, but Kathy insisted on opening gifts on Christmas Eve instead. None of the other kids objected.

"Kath, I thought Brian and Lauren still believed in Santa Claus?" Dan whispered. "Aren't they going to be suspicious about opening their gifts before Santa arrives on Christmas morning?"

"Dan, you should really spend more time at home. The twins are almost nine. They agreed to sit on Santa's lap this year so you could take your annual photos, but if you think they still believe in Santa Claus, they are really pulling your chain, hon."

Not surprisingly, the gift opening started off more somber than in other years. In fact, with the events of the week, Kathy had no chance to do her last minute shopping and the number of gifts per child was a little slim. Dan's mom recognized this and did some last minute shopping to buy some smaller gifts for each of her grandchildren in order to achieve some semblance of normality. As had become the custom after her husband Ed passed away, she would join her son's family on Christmas Eve and play Santa Claus — allowing each child to open just one present. Today, she was given the task of distributing *all* the gifts. Of all people, it was Michael who tried hardest to maintain a festive spirit. Once again, Dan found Michael's demeanor to be infectiously positive.

"Hey, grandma, don't start with the presents until we turn on some Christmas music." He went to his father's CD player and put on an old Burl Ives collection of Christmas songs, beginning with *"Have a Holly Jolly Christmas!"* Indeed, Michael succeeded in lifting everyone's mood. In no time at all, Tom, Brian, and Lauren were buzzing about their gifts as though it was a normal Christmas.

Kathy's intuition about celebrating early was on the mark. Following dinner, Michael said he felt chilled and Dan took his temperature — 102. He called the nurse practitioner on-call as Sampson had instructed him to do if Michael spiked a fever, but he already knew that she would demand that Michael return to the hospital for blood cultures. It would be the first of many sets of blood cultures. Dan was only thankful that the blood specimens could be drawn through one of the Broviac catheters, without the need for multiple venipunctures.

In the five days following Black Monday, most family members and friends became aware of the Ulek situation in one way or another. On several occasions, Dan took the phone off the hook to postpone dealing with well-wishers. *Seems like bad things always happen to good people. Let us know if there is anything we can do. Just so you know, we are all in total shock. We wanted to let you know that you're in our thoughts. We'll be praying for you.* It was all very sincere and thoughtful — but it got old fast, and after a while, the phone calls and voicemails just served to re-create the pain.

What Dan did appreciate were the warm meals that neighbors and friends dropped by each day — all organized by Louise Richert. Kathy was in no mood to cook during that week before Christmas, and during the next three months, she would spend long hours in the hospital. So the prepared meals were a huge help for the entire family.

Dan occasionally would spend the night in Michael's hospital room. But Kathy bore most of night duty — typically staying until mid-afternoon when Dan would create time to spell her.

Dan continued working full-time as he had promised himself. It helped to take his mind off Michael's condition. As he dealt with the entire ordeal, he often thought that dealing with a sick child would alter his approach to his own patients. *Maybe that would be a good thing. Maybe my understanding of patient's needs and fears — my empathy for them — has been shadowed by my academic ambitions.*

But the ordeal with his son sometimes had the opposite effect. *You think you're sick? Try having acute myelogenous leukemia! Listen, you may be sick, but you're not dying! Can't afford your medications? Come take a look at my medical bills!*

In early January, Michael developed persistent fever and a new cough. At this point, his blood counts were all low as expected from the chemotherapy, and he was requiring platelet transfusions about every three days to prevent spontaneous bleeding. Friends, family members and complete strangers from St. Rita's parish generously donated platelets and other blood products to the CMC blood bank when word got out about Michael's predicament. *Someday, we'll have to deal with a long list of thank-you cards.* Although all of his cultures were negative to date, he was treated with broad spectrum antibiotics because his nearly nonexistent white blood cell count posed a risk of spontaneous bacterial infections.

After Michael was on antibiotics for four days, Sue Sampson arranged to meet both Kathy and Dan after her morning rounds.

"Michael's chest x-ray yesterday showed bilateral lung infiltrates – shadows on the x-ray suggesting persistent pneumonia. He's not responding to the current antibiotics and he still has a fever. My bigger concern is that his pulse ox is marginal." It was rare for Sampson to slip into medical lingo when addressing Kathy, so it was clear to Kathy that Sue was seriously concerned.

"I'm sorry?" said Kathy

"His oxygen levels are abnormally low, despite giving him more and more oxygen through that cannula around his nose. We need to perform a bronchoscopy pretty urgently to determine if Michael has some unusual infection warranting more specific therapy."

Dan was fully aware of the routine. He also dealt with immunosuppressed patients at risk for infection and agreed that a very aggressive approach was necessary when his patients developed fever and pulmonary infiltrates.

But he was now acutely aware of how different it felt to be on the patient's side of the fence. He had never been a patient himself, but through Michael, he vicariously experienced the helplessness of being hospitalized, lying in bed and being told what was going to happen next, what medications he needed to take, what side effects he would experience, what pain and suffering were necessary to assure an outcome sometimes of more importance to the doctor than to the patient. He found himself internally rebelling. *Why don't we just wait a day or so and see if the antibiotics take effect? Why don't we add anti-fungal antibiotics empirically? Can't we just wait and see what happens?*

But he realized that Sampson was correct and resisted the temptation to be either the patient himself or his son's doctor. The bronchoscopy, allowing direct visualization of the pulmonary tree through an endoscopy tube passed down the trachea, was necessary to examine Michael's airways, to take culture samples from deep within the lungs, and to biopsy suspicious looking tissue.

"When and where?" he asked.

"Just to be cautious, I am moving Michael to the Peds ICU and it will get done this afternoon. Pulmonary wants to intubate him for the procedure and hopefully extubate him immediately afterwards. What happens after that depends on the findings from the bronch."

Hopefully extubate him? Dan suddenly had a flashback to his residency experience. Intubation and placement on a ventilator was the beginning of the end for most of his leukemic patients back then. Respiratory failure was ominous. Once the patient was intubated with an endotracheal tube in their throat, they could not speak.

Michael may never speak to us again.

Dan was wrong. Michael tolerated the bronchoscopy well, was immediately extubated and transferred back to the floor. From Michael's point of view, the procedure was a delightful experience. He was sedated with ketamine, just as he was for the bone marrow biopsy. Ketamine is a short-acting sedative with both narcotic and hallucinogenic effects. It was a favorite drug used to provide short-acting "twilight" anesthesia for minor procedures on children, such as bone marrow biopsies, lumbar punctures or "spinal taps," and biopsies of other solid organs. Basically, getting IV ketamine was like a fifteen minute acid trip with an added heroin rush.

As the ketamine wore off, Michael woke up but was actively hallucinating. "Dad, your watch is on fire! And it smells really bad. Your watch is sending signals to Mom. I don't think Mom is receiving."

"We're here, Michael. Come back to earth," said Kathy.

Indeed Michael had, in just a few weeks, developed a fondness for a number of drugs. Ketamine was for special occasions — bone marrow biopsies and other procedures. He became an expert on available sleeping pills and their respective doses. His favorite drug was Demerol, which was often given as part of a cocktail to prevent transfusion reactions. It was particularly good when administered intravenously. In weeks to come, it would be given in higher doses to alleviate pain.

Dan often joked, "Dude, we're gonna cure your leukemia and end up with a junkie on our hands!" *That's a scenario I would happily accept.*

During those nights he spent with Michael at the hospital, Dan would order hot dogs and fries from the hospital menu (Michael had virtually no interest in any other item on the menu), watch some TV, then play some rock & roll tunes on his portable CD player as bedtime came closer. Staying overnight had some benefits as Dan could actually wake up late, take a shower in Michael's room, and be in his office or on rounds within a few minutes as the adult hospital was connected to Children's and his office was two minutes away. And he was sure that nobody noticed that he would wear the same set of clothes for two consecutive days. *Or did they?*

As they listened to music together late at night, Dan encouraged Michael to think about the leukemic cells dying in his blood and bone marrow. "Don't talk out loud, just think about the chemotherapy working and killing the bad cells." Dan wasn't sure where all of this came from. His religious beliefs had waned even before Michael's illness, but he always believed that every physical illness was influenced by psychological factors that he didn't pretend to understand. As Dan fell asleep on the parents' roll-out bed listening to M.C. Hammer ("*Can't Touch This!*"), he internally hummed his mantra *(Leukemia cells: Die!)* Two hours later, he was awakened by the familiar sounds of Michael retching and vomiting, chatting with the night nurse, and asking for more Demerol. "Can we try upping it a milligram or two this time?"

Two days later, Michael deteriorated and was transferred back to the PICU because of worsening respiratory failure. Sue Sampson was out of town and her junior partner, Patricia Dean, called Dan and Kathy to meet urgently. She was older than Sue, her graying hair was tied in a long pony tail, and she wore round, wire-rim glasses – like John Lennon spectacles – and a necklace of multi-colored beads. *Ex-hippy.*

"We need to re-intubate Michael and provide ventilator assistance. Not only is his oxygenation deteriorating but he is retaining CO_2 as well."

Kathy immediately disliked Dr. Dean, as much for her negative aura as for her inability to talk down to a lay person. *I'm sure that Dan understands all this, but I am an ex-dietician housewife!*

"Most of the bronchoscopy results are back. I'm sorry that Dr. Sampson is not in town to tell you all of this, but it appears that Michael's pulmonary infiltrates are leukemic infiltrates. Some special stains are pending, but the pathologist is convinced that we are dealing with leukemic infiltration. This is an uncommon complication, but frankly, I've never seen a patient survive when the leukemic cells have infiltrated the lungs in this way. In other words, it's a uniformly fatal complication. Dr. and Mrs. Ulek, I am seriously suggesting that you call it quits before we re-intubate your son and prolong his misery. I am recommending comfort measures only."

After a long pause, Kathy spoke first. "No way. Intubate Michael if necessary and keep him alive until his real doctor returns. With all due respect, Dr. Dean, we are meeting you for the first time and I will simply not give up based on your one-day review of the information."

"What special stains were you talking about?" asked Dan.

"Pneumocystis, Cytomegalovirus, Cryptococcus, other fungal stains, but Dr. Ulek, the pathologists really don't think —"

"I agree with my wife — and let's hear about the special stains before we declare my son dead."

Michael may never speak to us again.

Dr. Dean now focused her gaze on Dan, refusing to look Kathy in the eyes again. "All right, but I've discussed the case with Radiation Therapy. We plan to irradiate Michael's left lung tonight. There is some data suggesting that this provides palliation for leukemic infiltrates — but I emphasize, Dr. Ulek — palliation, not cure."

As it turned out, the decision to re-intubate Michael was not an elective matter requiring parental consent. As they returned to the PICU from their meeting with Dr. Dean, Dan and Kathy immediately noted a flurry of activity near Michael's isolation room. Dan, heart sinking even further than it had during the unpleasant meeting with Dr. Dean, quickly recognized the "code cart" outside the room. The scene was nightmarish as they saw Michael, his bed, and the wall next to his hospital bed covered with blood. The PICU fellow quickly whisked them to an area outside of Michael's room.

"What the hell happened?" asked Dan. "We were only gone for twenty minutes."

"Massive hemoptysis." He nodded to Kathy, "Coughing up bright red blood. I've never seen anything like it. He literally had projectile hemoptysis, coughing blood up against the wall, against me, coughing up blood everywhere. We called a code and we had to intubate him to tamponade the bleeding site — presumably a bronchial artery — and right now it seems to have worked. I guess the leukemic infiltrates eroded into a bronchial artery. I'm sure he lost half of his blood volume, Dr. Ulek. We got him typed and crossed for five units — he may need more. I didn't even know you were here. I'm really sorry, Dr. Ulek."

"Sorry?" said Kathy. "You just saved my son's life. And you know what? He's gonna wake up to thank you himself."

As she was speaking, Kathy immediately recognized Father Jim, a parish priest from St. Rita's, walking into the PICU. He only vaguely recognized Kathy and Dan and quickly explained that he was called by a nursing supervisor to administer the Last Rights to Michael.

Kathy was shocked. *No, no, no. Michael is not dying. I hate Dr. Dean, I hate the nursing supervisor, and I hate you, Father Jim.*

With no further discussion, Father Jim methodically proceeded with the sacramental ceremony, anointing Michael's hands and feet, forgiving his sins, and commending his soul to heaven. Kathy felt ill and left the room.

Michael did not die that day. His condition stabilized, but he remained intubated, sedated and unable to communicate with the outside world for the next six weeks.

Word about Michael's Last Rights spread quickly throughout St. Rita's parish community and throughout the Ulek's neighborhood in Solon. Louise Richert worked quickly with Father Jim and arranged a special evening Mass for the sick. Dan offered to stay with Michael that night so Kathy could attend the Mass. The church was packed — on a weekday night. Kathy was emotionally overwhelmed by the outpouring of parishioners, including many complete strangers who were moved by the story of a young parishioner stricken by an awful disease. The event strengthened Kathy's belief in the healing power of prayer.

Susan Sampson returned two days later and called Dan and Kathy for yet another meeting to discuss Michael's condition.

"The special stains have come back from the bronchoscopy and revealed invasive Aspergillosis, a serious fungal infection."

"So they were wrong about leukemic infiltrates in the lungs? They radiated his lungs for three days for no good reason?" asked Kathy.

"Yes, they were wrong about leukemic infiltrates, but Kathy, this is a seriously bad infection as I'm sure Dan knows. We will begin treatment with intravenous amphotericin immediately, but in my experience, Michael's best chance for fighting this infection relies on his white blood cell count normalizing. His counts have been close to zero the past few days."

"Can you transfuse him with white blood cells?" asked Kathy.

"Good question. White cell transfusions were used routinely at one time but never proved to be effective in preventing or treating infections. We are giving him a relatively new granulocyte stimulating factor, but it will only be effective if the donor cells have successfully engrafted within Michael's marrow. I'm afraid the best treatment for his low white count right now is tincture of time."

Dan took another turn staying with Michael that night. His son was intubated and heavily sedated, but Dan still played some rock and roll music on the CD player — this time choosing some early Beatles' songs — and gently whispered into Michael's ear:

Bad cells die, good cells live! They were listening to "You Can't Do That" and "Run For Your Life."

Well, at least Dan was listening.

It was almost 9:00 p.m. and Dan was surprised when Sue Sampson returned for a nocturnal visit. "Burning the midnight oil, Susan?"

"I was called in urgently to see another patient and thought I'd stop by to say hello. Can I have a word with you outside?"

They stepped into the work area outside Michael's ICU room and Susan went on, "Dan, do you remember the construction that was occurring on the fourth floor when you first admitted Michael to Children's CMC before Christmas?"

"Yes, renovation of the new pediatric wing. Why?"

"It's well known that the incidence of Aspergillus infection rises exponentially when immunosuppressed patients are housed near construction sites of that kind. The mold is literally shaken out of the walls and becomes airborne. Standard ventilation units are not sufficient to clear the airborne spores. Long before I met Michael, I argued with the hospital that I wanted my patients temporarily housed in the adult hospital until the construction was completed — but my plea fell on deaf ears."

Why is she telling me this?

"I'm not really sure why I'm telling you this, but I wanted you to know."

Damn hospital administrators cutting corners again to preserve their precious bottom line.

In the next three weeks, Michael required multiple surgical procedures. The Aspergillus infection evolved into a fungus ball in his left lung — literally like a ball of mold on an old piece of bread — and he underwent a lobectomy on his left lower lobe. He came out of that surgery with two chest tubes inserted into the pleural space around his left lung, each designed to drain infected fluid into a bag hanging at his bedside. With the chest tubes, the Broviac catheters and a Foley catheter in his bladder, Michael was literally bound by plastic to his ICU bed.

Later that week, he developed fungal pericarditis — an infection of the lining around his heart. This progressed rapidly to pericardial tamponade — a condition in which fluid build-up in that cardiac lining becomes so massive that it suffocates the heart, preventing its normal contractions. He required urgent middle-of-the-night surgery for a pericardial drainage and stripping — removal of the normal lining around his heart to allow drainage of the infected fluid. From this new incision, another plastic drain was added for several days.

In working up his recurrent fevers, an abdominal CT scan revealed a fungus ball — Aspergillus again — in the upper pole of his right kidney. The presence of the fungal infection in multiple organs prompted Sue Sampson to conclude that the Aspergillus had become blood borne — disseminating throughout Michael's body at some point — and hopefully controlled now by the amphotericin, a powerful antifungal drug. Peds Urology was asked to perform a hemi-nephrectomy, in which only the diseased part of a kidney is removed while leaving behind as much normal tissue as possible. Jack Lederman was the surgeon and was nationally renowned for his work in pediatric hemi-nephrectomies. It was supposed to be a two-hour procedure. Six hours after sending Michael off for yet another surgery, Lederman came to the waiting room to tell Dan and Kathy that everything went smoothly.

"Smoothly? We've been waiting here for half a day, thinking the worst."

"Oh, just some routine OR delays."

Just the way things work at an academic medical center.

"Everything went smoothly and your son will be fine from a urologic point of view. As far as I could tell, it was a single isolated fungus ball and the remainder of the kidney looked normal."

Dan wondered whether three courses of radiation therapy helped to promote the spread of the fungal infection. In addition to the major surgeries, Michael had two more bone marrow biopsies performed at his bedside as part of the routine bone marrow transplant protocol.

The series of events left Dan and Kathy numb.

One ramification of Michael's prolonged hospitalization was that it forced Dan to bond with his other three children while Kathy spent her evenings and nights at CMC-Children's. Each of them had grown a bit older rather quickly during the prolonged winter months. Dan tried to maintain some semblance of normality and, perhaps for the first time, took some serious interest in the kids' school work and extracurricular activities. Tom was now a thirteen-year-old adolescent and Dan awkwardly attempted to discuss girls and other issues of pubertal importance, coming just shy of a traditional birds-and-bees talk. If Tom was anything like Dan was at the age of thirteen, it was likely that he could probably teach his father a few things about sex anyhow. The twins were industrious fourth-graders who brought homework from St. Rita's each weekday night. Dan found that he actually enjoyed helping them get through it and was proud that he could still handle fourth-grade material. Of course, each evening at dinner there was a discussion about Michael's status. Sue Sampson suggested that it might be too traumatic to let the siblings see their brother while he was sedated and intubated, so Dan and Kathy provided daily updates as an alternative. Even Dan did his best to be optimistic and hopeful for the sake of Tom, Lauren, and Brian.

During this time, Kathy developed a special bond with Father Jim despite the angry Last Rights encounter. His homily was inspiring at the Mass for the sick, invoking faith in God's healing powers. Father Jim visited Michael in the hospital virtually every day, except for Sundays when he was busy with Masses at St. Rita's. Dan was rarely around during these morning meetings and only years later would Kathy share that, above and beyond his religious connections, Father Jim provided a special element of personal friendship that helped her get through the ordeal. Although Kathy was a practicing Catholic before Michael's illness, she subsequently became a *devout* Catholic. *I bet she'll start going to Mass on vacations now — IF we ever vacation again.* From a distance, Dan greatly appreciated Father Jim's support, but in contrast to his wife, struggled to translate that appreciation into a religious conviction. For many years thereafter, Father Jim was a regular invitee to social events at the Ulek household. Kathy loved the idea. Dan basically tolerated it. He liked Father Jim, but he was not a fan of his holy Church.

Whether or not it was God's will, Michael slowly improved and during the last week of February, was extubated. Kathy and Dan could not wait to talk to Michael — to converse with their son, and share their thoughts, their fears, and their hopes.

It would take a while longer. Michael had been sedated with propafol for six weeks. The drug was slowly weaned to facilitate his extubation. When Michael awoke, he was completely psychotic. While he didn't recognize his mother or father, he did once again recognize Dan's watch, noting that it was expelling a green gas that was somehow depleting the planet's energy sources.

Peds Psychiatry was consulted and assured Dan and Kathy that this was a common and quickly reversible form of psychosis. He improved dramatically with haloperidol, an anti-psychotic agent.

One morning, Michael woke up his mother who was sleeping on the cot next to his PICU bed. "Mom, I just saw an angel. He didn't have wings but I knew right away he was an angel. He was a beautiful man with long blond hair, wearing a white suit, white shirt, white tie, and white shoes. As he walked, he was covered by a very bright light, like a spotlight from heaven. He touched me on the forehead and shoulder and told me not to worry about a thing. He just left. I wanted you see to see him. He was beautiful, Mom, the most beautiful man I've ever seen."

Kathy had been startled from her sleep but quickly relaxed. She had been taught and still believed that every human being is assigned a Guardian Angel that follows the person throughout his or her life. *This is not psychosis. This is real. An angel from heaven. Michael's Guardian Angel.* She hugged her son and kissed him.

A week later, Sue Sampson met with Dan and Kathy to deliver good news. "Michael's counts are normalizing and the most recent bone marrow biopsy shows no blasts. Folks, Michael

Ulek is in remission. Under normal circumstances, we would recommend a second round of chemotherapy in another week or two to assure complete eradication of the leukemic bone marrow. But with Michael's series of infectious complications, I'm concerned that he might not survive another round of chemo. I am recommending that we proceed with the bone marrow transplant as soon as possible."

"It's a miracle, Dr. Sampson," Kathy smiled. *God sent an angel to deliver a miracle to my son.*

The next day, Dan met with a CMC financial counselor, Arlene Brooks, to begin the process of dealing with the avalanche of medical bills that were beginning to arrive at home. Based on Arlene's recommendations from an earlier phone call, he put all of his bills to date in a file (actually a large paper bag) and brought them to her for this preliminary meeting. *If I don't understand these bills, how does the average Joe even stand a chance?* In contrast to *average Joe*, Dan benefited from the fact that most of the pediatric physicians and surgeons caring for Michael declared "insurance only" on their charge tickets — not exactly "professional courtesy" (i.e., free care offered from one physician to another) but basically an agreement not to collect any amount of the charge above and beyond what the insurance company agreed to pay. What insurance companies agreed to pay was sometimes only a small percentage of the actual charges from the physician. Over the years, professional practices learned the game — increase charges to some outrageous amount, understanding that they would collect only a small fraction of the charges. The problem was that many families then got a bill to cover the balance of the charge after the sometimes pitiful coverage by the insurance company — unless the hospital or the physician agreed to accept insurance only. Unfortunately, many of the ancillary professional services involved in Michael's care — Radiology, Anesthesiology, Respiratory Therapy to name a few — did *not* accept insurance only. Dan became increasingly concerned that the uncovered portions of Michael's medical bills would drive him to bankruptcy.

Arlene was a pleasant and attractive middle-age African American woman, probably in her early fifties. After spending twenty minutes trying to organize the pile of bills and papers, she spoke up. "You need to apply for Medicaid to cover some of the charges not covered by your private insurance."

"Sure," said Dan, presuming that she was kidding. "I am almost clueless about medical insurance and medical bills, but I have lots of Medicaid patients and I know that Medicaid applies only to the unemployed or disabled."

"No, there are some exceptions, and Michael qualifies because technically he has been institutionalized for more than six weeks."

"Institutionalized?"

"Being housed in an intensive care unit for more than six weeks qualifies as being institutionalized."

"Incredible — so what do we need to do?"

"You'll need to go to the Welfare Office and apply for Medicaid. The sooner the better so I can start dealing with this big paper bag of yours."

Dan went to the Welfare Office the next day; it was just a half mile down Euclid Avenue from the CMC, near the border of Cleveland and East Cleveland. As was his daily custom, he was wearing a sport coat and tie. When he spotted the people in line ahead of him, he decided to lose the tie. *I am the only Caucasian here.* He waited almost an hour before getting to the front desk.

"I'm here to apply for Medicaid." The Hispanic receptionist looked him up and down and smiled.

"Fill out this form and return it to me. Take your time and make sure that you use black ink only."

"You mean I have to go back to the end of the line?"

She answered affirmatively with an unfriendly smile.

The form was simple enough, mostly demographic information — age, gender, marital status, etc. — and then a few lines asking for information about annual income before taxes, total assets, monthly expenses, and other sources of income. After another thirty minutes in line, he returned the form to the same receptionist whose eyes immediately scanned down to the financial data.

"Is this your idea of a joke?"

He looked into her eyes, took a deep breath, remained calm, and captured his thoughts before speaking.

Yes it is, honey. This whole thing is a miserable fucking joke. I have an innocent child who may die soon for no good reason and whose chances of surviving have been diminished by my entrusted hospital that showered him in bread mold and then negligently fried his lungs — all for fun! I am making it all up just to entertain the Welfare Department in general and you in particular! It looks like you needed a rise of some kind so I came to this ghetto unemployment office to entertain you. I am NOT unemployed — I am a rich doctor, facing destitution and bankruptcy. All of this is a miserable fucking joke — and I expect you to start laughing.

"No, ma'am, it's no joke."

The next day, he left a bottle of his favorite white wine — a Cakebread chardonnay — for Arlene Brooks. Over the next few years, she got several bottles of chardonnay — maybe a whole case.

The bone marrow transplant was anti-climactic. Lauren was admitted to the hospital for one overnight stay and also received intravenous ketamine for the bone marrow harvest — about twenty punctures of her iliac crest to obtain about 150 milliliters of precious marrow. Later, she would share stories with her brothers about the marvels of ketamine. *Another junkie!* When the anesthesia wore off, there was considerable pain from the multiple punctures, but Lauren never complained — until years later, of course, when she enjoyed dramatizing the event. *Lauren, our drama queen.*

The bone marrow, looking much like regular blood drawn from a vein, was enriched with stem cells and other precursors of mature blood cells that would populate Michael's bone marrow. Kathy had envisioned that some kind of surgical procedure was required to inject Lauren's marrow into Michael's skeleton — maybe a bone graft of some sort from Lauren that was surgically implanted into one of Michael's arms or legs — or maybe his iliac crest. In fact, bone marrow "transplants" are performed by way of a simple transfusion of the blood/marrow — a plastic bag of red fluid hooked up to a standard IV line — in this case hooked up to one of Michael's Broviac catheters. Magically, the precursor cells enter the circulation and find their way home to the inner spaces of bones where, in successful cases, they engraft, proliferate and provide healthy cells for the circulation.

After a winter of countless blood product transfusions, unexpected complications, urgent operations, and near-death experiences, the bone marrow engrafted within three weeks. Shortly thereafter, his blood counts were close to normal and Michael felt well. There were no complications. All of Michael's infections had cleared and he was discharged home.

It was a miracle.

Twelve

Cote d'Azur —
October 1996

It was Dan's fifth trip to Europe but his first with Kathy. Most of his previous European excursions were short trips for single day meetings or talks. This trip was planned around a meeting of the International Lung and Heart Transplantation Society in Monaco, and Dan decided to add a week of vacation prior to the meeting. Michael's illness had eliminated any thoughts of long vacations for almost two years. Now Dan, but especially Kathy, needed and deserved some time alone — and everything that Dan had heard about the French Riviera (*the Cote d'Azur!*) convinced him that this would be a vacation to remember. "We're lucky that Mom is healthy and still willing to watch the kids," said Dan, trying to assure Kathy that Michael and the other children would be in good hands.

The trip from Cleveland to Newark to Nice, France went smoothly. Dan's airfare was covered by the ILHTS and he used frequent flyer miles to upgrade Kathy to business class. *She'll never agree to fly coach again.* On the trans-Atlantic segment, he took a sleeper after dinner and a couple of scotch-on-the-rocks and was able to sleep for almost four hours. Kathy was not accustomed to the overnight routine and struggled to catch a few winks. The plane landed in Nice just after dawn. The plan was to rent a car, spend two nights in Nice, then drive west for a three-day stay in Cannes, then drive back east to Monaco for the meeting where Dan was schedule to give three presentations — two talks and one poster.

International airports are configured differently than most US airports, but Dan wanted Kathy to think he new exactly what he was doing as they cleared customs and he struggled to identify signage for the rental car desks. *Why don't any of these people speak English?* When they finally reached the Hertz lot, they discovered that all cars in this part of France were the size of shoeboxes. Their little black and gray Renault was cute but just barely accommodated four suitcases — two in the trunk, and two in the back seat. Kathy carried Dan's heavy briefcase on her lap. She would have preferred a car with a bigger trunk so all the suitcases and carry-ons could be stored neatly in an organized fashion.

Dan's next challenge was re-discovering the stick shift. He had driven cars with stick shifts years ago — even managing to drive a stick shift Toyota through the hills of San Francisco during their honeymoon. But it was not like riding a bicycle — Dan was hoping for a little practice when he suddenly found himself on a busy road heading in the wrong direction and not quite certain how to shift into reverse. If it weren't for her jet lag *(my God, it's really only 2:00 a.m. on our clocks),* Kathy came close to making a comment about one's need to be smarter than a stick shift. Instead, she just mentally added this little misadventure to the list of stories she would use for some future marital tête-à-tête.

At this point in their lives, Dan and Kathy were still not affluent enough to afford five star hotels and settled instead for a pretty mediocre three-star place (read: running water, your own toilet, and of course the mysterious *bidet*) in Nice.

By the time they got to the hotel, it was almost 10:30 a.m. and Kathy felt like she was getting her second wind, anxious to do some sightseeing. Dan demanded that the only way to survive the first day in Europe was to head directly to bed, force oneself to sleep till the afternoon, and schedule an evening of light activities. The bed, which would be known as a "single bed" in the United States (about what college kids got in their dorms), was wedged snugly between three walls, so that bathroom calls required some acrobatic leapfrogging.

The plan for a late morning nap worked. That evening, Kathy and Dan leisurely strolled the streets surrounding their hotel in Nice and discovered French cheese — delectable, stinky, and *not pasteurized* — so much better than anything they had tasted back home. And everything in this part of the world was served with a bowl of green olives — "a la Nicois." For Dan, the other remarkable discovery was that it was almost impossible to find French Burgundy or Bordeaux wines in this part of France. He had only recently made an effort to collect a small cellar *(okay, a basement closet)* of California wines and didn't pretend to know anything about the wines of France — but he was at least aware of the two major red varietals. In Nice, the wine lists all exclusively featured the varietals of Au Provénce. He would scroll down the wine list and select a wine halfway between the cheapest and the most expensive — a trick that almost always worked when he was clueless about the selections. *Okay, not Bordeaux but very tasty. God, I love to travel.*

Dan and Kathy relaxed in Cannes. Their two-and-a-half star hotel was only a block away from the more famous (and unaffordable) Carlton Hotel that architecturally dominated the city's palm tree-lined seaside promenade. The hotel was more like a hotel-apartment and they could sit on their balcony and peer into the apartment-like homes of local citizens

going about their daily routines. Kathy noticed that, in contrast to American wives who typically shop for groceries once
a week, most French wives walked to markets on a daily basis
— sometimes twice daily — to buy the day's food. Maybe it
was inadequate storage or refrigerator space. Whatever — she
didn't spot many overweight people in the streets of southern
France. The local folks spent much of their time either walking
or bicycling as part of their daily routine. She wasn't going to
return home and re-invent the American way, but she did mentally commit herself to begin a regular walking program when
she got back to the United States.

They visited the Palais des Festivals, site of the annual film
festival, sampled some wines at a nearby vineyard, and bought
some French perfumes from one of the dozens of perfume fac-
tories just north of the city. They also happened upon their first-
ever topless beach just three blocks from their hotel.

"Go ahead, I dare you, Kath; take it off," urged Dan.

"From what I can see, most of the women here would be better off putting it back on."

She was right. For every buxom young gal baring her
breasts, there were at least ten topless ladies over the age of
sixty who needed bras much more than they needed tanned
titties. Still, the afternoon at the beach made Dan horny and,
following a dinner of fresh seafood at one of Cannes' many
open-air seaside restaurants, he was anxious to get Kathy back
to the hotel and in the sack.

The drive from Cannes to Monaco was mostly via the Grand
Corniche, the "highway" built by Napoleon, once known as the
Roman *Via Aurelia*, the route used by Roman legions marching
to and from Gaul. This "upper road" traversed the upper preci-
pices of the cliffs and steep slopes that run the gamut of the east-
ern section of the Cote d'Azur, providing breathtaking views of
the Mediterranean Sea to the south below and the posh villas to
the north of the Corniche — olive trees everywhere. It was on
the road connecting the Grand Corniche to Monaco that Princess
Grace died in a fiery car crash. The trip provided vistas distinct

from those offered by the Moyenne Corniche ("middle road") halfway down the slopes, or the Corniche inferieur ("lower road"), which was constructed many years post-Napoleon by the Prince of Monaco.

In need of lunch, they happened upon the village of Eze, one of a few medieval villages perched high above the sea along the Grand Corniche. As they traversed cobblestone walkways through small archways, they discovered *Le Jardin Exotique*, a lushly landscaped garden of cactus and other exotic plants. *Cactus plants in France?* They found the hotel Chateau Eza and its amazing restaurant positioned on balconies overlooking the Mediterranean Sea hundreds of feet below. *Man, I wish we could have afforded to stay here.*

Waiting for their wine to be served, Dan found himself staring at his wife against the background of Eze and the sea. "Do you realize that you are more beautiful now than you were when we got married?"

Kathy was caught pleasantly off-guard. "A penny for your *real* thoughts! Dan, this place is magnificent. Being here in Europe makes you think of the past and our ancestors, and these views are amazing. We are so lucky to be able to do this."

"It really *is* magnificent," Dan agreed. Look out there at those small fishing boats — probably bringing in tonight's supper for family and friends. The people here look so relaxed and carefree — none of the stresses we deal with in our lives back home. It makes you wonder how different things would be if we had been plucked into this kind of environment instead of the American mainstream." *So who exactly decides where one is plucked?*

Dan swirled around to take in the views from east to west. *This may be the most peaceful and most beautiful place in the world. I could live here.*

They ordered a light lunch consisting of a spinach salad, French bread with unsalted butter, French brie, and the ubiquitous bowl of sweet green olives on the side. The wine was a light and crisp Chablis from a regional vineyard — a perfect accompaniment to the warmed brie. It was a special afternoon. By

3:00 p.m., they realized that they had been enjoying their wine and cheese for more than two hours.

After lunch, they slowly headed back to their shoebox car, back through *Le Jardin Exotique*, shouldering their way through narrow streets with steep steps running by carefully restored houses — each with colorful fresh flowers in windows above the stream of tourists, travelers, and local citizens. *I could live here. I could retire here. I could live here until I die.*

Thirteen

*Rome and Florence —
March 1998*

Dan and Kathy decided to fly from Newark to Rome and spend two days there before taking a train to Florence for the Third International Cyclosporine Symposium. It was their first trip to Italy. They paid a relative fortune to spend two nights at the grand Excelsior Hotel located off the Via Veneto, perched above the Spanish steps and a short walking distance to the Roman Forum. Rome was fantastic: great food, fantastic history, and ancient architecture.

Dan knew that Kathy would especially love their first-ever visit to the Vatican. Unbelievably, the Sistine Chapel was *closed* on Monday — their only day to visit. *We get to Wally World and it's frickin' closed?* But walking through the immense Vatican Square and St. Peter's Basilica was still an incredible experience for each of them.

As they walked through the mammoth cathedral, Dan was particularly impressed with the many *open* confessionals offering confessions in many different languages throughout the church. *So many sins. So many sinners. Bless me father for I have sinned. My last confession was . . .* He recalled that his own last confession — ever — was during his junior year at Walsh Jesuit High School. The crazy Jesuit priests there had decided to go the open confession format — no sliding screen with shadowy images of the priest on the other side of the wall. No, an open confession in an open room, face-to-face with the same priests who served as his teachers, coaches, counselors, and — sometimes — friends. At this point in his life, he was no longer confessing disobedience or lying to Mom and Dad. *I am not going to tell my football coach face-to-face how many times I have masturbated since my last confession four weeks ago!* Another Catholic tradition ended at the age of sixteen.

His mind turned to Michael's near-death experience. While the experience increased Kathy's religious convictions, it *altered* Dan's. He still appreciated *good versus evil,* but he struggled with the concept of a single God, of sins and sinners, of heaven and hell and he became even less sure of an afterlife. *I have nothing to confess.* He always felt that he lived his life based on Christian principles, but his loyalty to formal religion in general, and to the Catholic Church in particular, had faded long ago. Still, he found himself catching yet another glimpse in the midst of St. Peter's. *What is it?*

After touring the Vatican, Dan and Kathy discovered the wonderful neighborhoods of Trestavere, a visually and gastronomically delightful section of the city. This was classic old Europe: narrowed streets emptying into broader *piazzas,* each dotted with cafes, bars, and sometimes small churches. In these quiet neighborhoods, tourists mingled with local citizens and the smart tourists would head for the cafes heavily occupied by the locals. The weather in Rome was unseasonably warm, and most of the restaurants had their outdoor cafes open and in full bloom. Good pasta. Great Italian wine. Dan enjoyed the Tuscany reds, but Kathy stuck with white pinot grigios as more than two glasses of red wine always gave her headaches and on a romantic night like this, she did not want to go to bed telling her husband that she had a headache.

Rome was fun but Florence was even more interesting. Smaller in size, equal in beauty but with a distinctly different personality and cuisine. Dan and Kathy were prepared for what the travelogues referred to as "art sickness" experienced by some visitors to this seat of the Renaissance. The large number of museums with original Renaissance paintings and sculpture was expected. But Dan and Kathy were surprised by the quantity and quality of *outdoor* art. Not only were many of the churches and other buildings designed or decorated by Michelangelo or Brunelleschi, but frescoes, paintings, and ornately sculptured doors adorned the outside walls of many buildings throughout the city. In the piazza outside the Uffizi gallery, there were a number of majestic sculptures including a replica of Michelangelo's *David* that Dan and Kathy initially mistook for the real thing. *I thought the "David" would draw bigger crowds.*

The Third International Cyclosporine Symposium was a four-day conference devoted to research presentations dealing mostly with the world's fifteen-year experience with cyclosporine in solid-organ transplantation. Dan recalled attending the first Cyclosporine Symposium in Houston back in the mid-1980s and reflected on the major progress that had been made in the field of organ transplantation since that time. Dan had been invited to the Third International Symposium to chair a session of abstract presentations and also to give a talk entitled "Prednisone withdrawal in heart transplant recipients receiving cyclosporine" — essentially summarizing data from a protocol that he and Jack Hurtuk had been using in Cleveland for several years. Both of these meeting obligations were scheduled for the second day of the conference. Because the weather was spectacular, Dan decided to play hooky on the first day and to take Kathy to see the real *David*, housed in the Accademia Gallery, within walking distance of their hotel. More than a few other meeting attendees had the same idea, and the wait in line to see the sculpture of sculptures was more than an hour.

The real David was substantially bigger than life size and a magnificent piece of art. The statue stands on a podium in the middle of a large museum chamber surrounded by other lesser pieces crafted by Michelangelo and other Renaissance artists, allowing visitors to walk in a circle to examine every crevice of David's nude body from the anterior, posterior and lateral points of view. The typical beholder ponders the beautiful sculpture while internally recalling the story of David and Goliath, noting the slingshot in David's hand.

As he eyed the sculpture, Dan had an overwhelming sense of his bonds to other humans, past and present — another glimpse of some strange reality. He had experienced it when he first saw the Great Wall of China, the Mona Lisa in the Louvre, the Blue Mosque in Istanbul, and more recently in Rome at St. Peter's Basilica and while walking through the ancient ruins of the Roman Forum: some mysterious sense of commonness — a common sense of beauty, creativity, and ingenuity.

In college, he had been infatuated with the writings of the Jesuit priest Teilhard de Chardin and became struck by the possibility that human beings may be evolving to some collective consciousness. *Maybe that's the life after death — a final realization that we all have a single, collective soul.* Looking into the sculpted eyes of David, he once again caught that fleeting glimpse — something he had experienced only on rare occasions as a child and young adult, but increasingly in the past few years And then the sudden realization that between these rare glimpses, he would experience long periods of time being — as the song goes — comfortably numb.

"It's gorgeous Dan. It's the most beautiful sculpture I've ever seen. Thank you for bringing me here. We are so lucky to be able to do this — Dan are you okay?"

He snapped out of it. "Oh yes, Kath, just comfortably numb." Her perplexed look reminded him that she didn't recognize the song.

They lunched at an outdoor café near the Domo — the city's main church. Compared to Rome, the pastas were more delicate and served *al dente*. The tomato sauces were lighter and more akin to marinara. On the walk back to the hotel, half drunk after sharing a bottle of white wine, they stopped in one of the many warehouse-like leather shops in an alley of Florence's "leather district." Kathy bought not one, not two, but three leather jackets, including one for Lauren. *Like a kid in a candy store.* Dan was more than happy to oblige because he knew that he would be paid back with some "afternoon delight" when they returned to their hotel.

As an invited speaker and session chair, Dan was invited to a dinner with the meeting organizers and other speakers on the second night of the conference. He much preferred quiet dinners alone with his wife, but attending these formal dinners was a necessary part of maintaining an international academic reputation and rubbing shoulders with giants in the field. Kathy actually loved these kinds of social events and had a talent for mingling with total strangers and engaging them in conversations about spouses, families, and other topics that removed their thoughts from medicine, surgery, and transplantation. As expected for a group dinner of more than two hundred people, the food was prepared *en masse* and was mediocre — "surf and turf" — an overdone piece of salmon, a sinfully overdone chunk of "beef," and cold peas followed by a sticky chocolate parfait. But with Kathy's help, Dan made it through the affair. After dinner, the group was taken on a special tour of a normally hidden hallway in the Ponte Vecchio — an art gallery of sorts traversing the entire length of the bridge — and containing literally thousands of portraits by Renaissance noblemen. It wasn't true *art sickness*, but it was boring as hell.

As they walked back to their hotel, Dan and Kathy discussed the possibility of playing hooky again the next day, renting a car, and taking a drive to Tuscany: a morning drive and an afternoon of wine and cheese. Or maybe a side trip to Pisa or Sedona. Word was that the good weather was going to hold up so it would a nice day for a drive through Italian wine country.

Their hotel had the European tradition of checking room keys at the front desk whenever guests were leaving or returning. The bellman handed Dan the room key and a written message:

From: Rose Ulek
Re: Call home immediately about Michael

Dan's heart sank as he showed Kathy the message.

"Probably just checking about a sleepover or some school project — Dan, he has been in perfect health recently."

In their room, Dan immediately called the hotel operator to set up the overseas call. "Almost midnight here, should be dinner time back home — Mom's probably fixing supper."

Brian answered the phone.

"Hello from Italy, Brian! Mom and I are having a great time in Florence. Can I speak to Grandma?"

"Grandma's not here, Dad. She took Michael to the hospital right after we got home from school."

"To the CMC? What's wrong?"

"I don't know Dad. Michael stayed home from school today. Grandma said he has the flu or something. She called and left this number to call her at the hospital."

"Okay, Brian. Are you guys being good? I'll call Grandma and Mom will probably call you guys again tomorrow."

"What is it, Dan?" asked Kathy.

He started dialing the Children's CMC while answering. "Michael is in the hospital. Probably just the flu. I'm sure Mom was just being cautious."

"Michael Ulek's room."

"Mom?"

"Oh Dan, thank goodness you got my message."

"What's going on, Mom?"

"Michael was fine yesterday but he didn't go to school today, complaining of pain in his right leg."

"Pain in his leg? Did he sprain an ankle or something?"

"No, nothing of the sort that he could remember. But then he started throwing up and he felt hot. Temperature was 103. I called that Dr. Sampson's number and her nurse answered and told me to bring Michael to CMC for a direct admission."

Dan paused, trying to assimilate the facts and to consider diagnostic possibilities. Most people with the flu did not have isolated pain in one leg. *What's the connection between leg pain and fever? Deep vein thrombophlebitis? Cellulitis? In a 15-year-old boy?*

"Mom, can I speak to Michael?"

"He's not in the room. He's down getting an x-ray or some kind of scan. Dan — they think his leukemia has come back."

Leg pain — fever — leukemia? After four years of remission?

"Is Dr. Sampson there, Mom?"

"It's close to seven o'clock here and I think she's gone for the day. Should I get her office number for you?"

"No, don't bother — we'll catch the next flight home. We'll call you when we get in to the Newark airport."

Years later, Kathy and Dan would talk about their shortened trip to Florence. They recalled the symposium, the art, the great food and wine, the leather shops, the *David* but neither of them could recall the dreadful flight back to the US — couldn't recall how they made the hurried arrangements for the early return flight, couldn't remember the two hour train ride back from Florence to Rome, couldn't remember eating or drinking, couldn't remember if they spoke to each other at all during the eight-and-a-half-hour flight across the Atlantic.

Dan dialed the CMC number from Newark even before going through customs. He was surprised when Michael answered.

"Hi Dad. My leukemia's back. I figured as much." He sounded remarkably calm. Dan had hoped that in the past eight hours, better news would have emerged. *Just the flu. Nothing serious. Only a virus. A sprained ankle.*

"I'm gonna need more chemo, but they're talking about amputating my leg; that's what scares me a little."

Dan was scared, too, but completely confused. *Why would a relapse of leukemia lead to the need for amputating a limb?*

"The doctors are waiting for you to get here to give permission. Are you at home in Solon?"

Dan collected himself in an effort to sound unalarmed. "No, we just arrived in Newark from Rome. We should be back in Cleveland by 3:30 p.m. Tell your nurse that we'll be there around 4:30, okay? We'll be there as soon as we can Michael. Mom says hello, and we love you."

In contrast to the flight across the Atlantic Ocean, Dan vividly recalled the discussion with Kathy on the shorter trip from Newark to Cleveland. "I can't believe his leukemia has relapsed," Dan started. "It's been almost four years since the bone marrow transplant. Most cancers are considered to be cured after five years of remission. We were so close. He seemed to be healthy one week ago." *Did I miss the signs and symptoms once again?*

"Dan, please stop being Mr. Doom and Gloom — *Doctor* Doom and Gloom. I am no happier about this than you are, but we've been through it before and we will get through it again."

Dan wanted to tell Kathy that the prognosis of relapsing AML was miserably bad, but he knew it would serve little purpose with his ever-optimistic spouse. More importantly, he decided not to tell Kathy about the amputation, largely because he had no clue why it was being considered and was secretly hoping that this was some crazy misunderstanding on Michael's part. As they sped from Hopkins Airport up I-71 toward downtown Cleveland, Dan silently wondered. *Why is this happening to us? What kind of God would allow an innocent boy to be afflicted with such an awful disease? Did it serve some purpose in the move toward a collective consciousness?*

When they got to Michael's room, Sue Sampson was sitting on the edge of Michael's bed. She got up and introduced Alan Wilkinson, a senior pediatric vascular surgeon who Dan knew by reputation only.

Sue Sampson spoke first. "Michael's AML has relapsed. We haven't done a bone marrow biopsy yet, but his peripheral smear shows 30 percent blasts and his total white blood cell count is almost 70,000. We didn't see this kind of leukocytosis when he was first diagnosed four years ago but it's irrelevant — we simply need to initiate therapy as soon as possible. He'll need another bone marrow biopsy tonight and at least one more round of chemotherapy."

"But what's going on with his leg?" asked Dan.

Kathy glared at Dan and then at the vascular surgeon, angrily appreciating that something was being hidden from her. She knew that a normal white blood cell count was around 9,000 and that Michael's was very high. She also knew all about blasts and relapses, but nobody had told her anything about his leg.

Sue Sampson stood up and removed the bed covers from Michael's bare legs. The left leg looked normal. The right leg had a peculiar blue-black appearance from the knee down.

"What the heck?" asked Dan, baffled and shocked. *Looks like an arterial thrombosis in a seventy-year-old smoker with severe atherosclerosis.*

"We immediately consulted Alan because I've never seen anything like this in a patient with AML," said Susan.

Dr. Wilkinson cleared his throat and spoke up. "Hi, Alan Wilkinson." He was a bit rotund with thinning red hair and some beads of sweat on his upper lip. He had a distinctly British accent, or maybe South African.

"Our immediate concern was a vascular thrombosis or blood clot. We ordered Doppler studies and the large arteries are patent. In fact, Michael has palpable pulses in the foot. I saw this once as a fellow years ago — in an adult at Oxford. Leukemic microthrombi in small vessels, like microscopic aggregations of leukemic white blood cells. The net effect is the same as a clot in a major artery — severe ischemia ultimately resulting in gangrene."

Dan reached down to feel Michael's lower right leg. It was ice cold.

Wilkinson went on, "Earlier today we took the liberty of sending Michael for radiation therapy — essentially radiating the entire right leg. In your absence, we obtained administrative consent for the radiation because, in my opinion, this is a life-threatening emergency. We plan another round of radiation tomorrow morning. If he continues to show mottling of the skin or any new signs of tissue necrosis, I would recommend above-the-knee amputation as early as tomorrow — that's what we did for that Oxford patient during my fellowship."

"And he survived?" asked Dan.

"Can we move to the hallway, please?" Kathy demanded angrily.

"How dare you talk about *survival* in front of my son? I will *not* give permission for an amputation. We've been through this before and we will get through it again. The radiation will work. Now if you please, I'd like to have a few moments alone with Michael."

Dan found himself staring blankly at Sue Sampson and Alan Wilkinson.

"Well — I guess we have a plan."

Kathy stayed the night; having her luggage in the car from the trip to Italy made that easy. She insisted that Dan return home to spell his mother and to do his best to explain things to the other kids. Strangely, Michael's leg was not painful and he slept peacefully. Kathy did not sleep. She prayed.In the early morning, before sunrise and before Michael arose from his sleep, Kathy slipped the bed covers off his right leg. It appeared entirely normal. She turned on a night light to inspect his leg more closely. Again, the blue-black appearance had disappeared. Without waking Michael, she gently touched his leg. It was warm — the same warm feeling as his left leg. She suddenly had a powerful sense of another presence in the room. *The angel from heaven — Michael's Guardian Angel — had returned.*

Fourteen

Cleveland Medical Center — April 1998

Susan Sampson reasoned that Michael's leukemic white blood cells were extremely radiosensitive and that the leukemic infiltrates in his leg had dissipated after a single treatment with radiation. Kathy new better. *It was another miracle.* The amputation was not needed.

The treatment of Michael's relapse went pretty smoothly. A new Broviac catheter. Serial bone marrow biopsies. *Love that ketamine!* Bouts of nausea and vomiting from the chemotherapy. Lots of blood cultures and prophylactic antibiotics. *We've been through this before.*

Michael was fond of Beck's album, *Odelay* and that was the mainstay of late-night rock and roll entertainment that Dan and

Michael needed to deal with this relapse. Michael, bald once again from the chemotherapy, particularly liked "Devil's Haircut." Within two months of initiating chemotherapy, Michael was again in remission.

Sue Sampson called for another meeting with Dan and Kathy.

"Now that Michael is in remission, we need to discuss the next steps. The original bone marrow transplant from Lauren lasted almost four years but ultimately failed. I don't think it would be wise to repeat another conventional transplant after this relapse."

Dan was confused as he and Kathy had presumed that another transplant would be performed. "But you've said that transplant offers the best chance," he said.

"Technology has advanced since Michael was first diagnosed four years ago. I've been talking with colleagues in Seattle. In similar cases, they have had some success using activated T-lymphocytes from HLA identical donors. We would use Lauren as the donor, but instead of aspirating her bone marrow, we'd obtain peripheral blood — a simple blood draw — extract the T-lymphocytes and grow them in a culture medium exposed to high concentrations of IL-2."

"Interleukin-2?" asked Dan. He was aware of this important cytokine that served as a growth factor for lymphocytes. In fact, the major effect of cyclosporine was to block the generation of IL-2, preventing full activation of T-cells and thus preventing rejection of a transplanted organ.

"Yes, interleukin-2. Then after a few days, when the T-cells are proliferating rapidly and really angry, we infuse them into Michael's peripheral blood, hoping for an anti-leukemic effect — Lauren's T-cells killing Michael's leukemic cells. The real promise of the technique is the possibility that some of the activated T-cells will develop into *memory* cells that may persist for a long duration — perhaps indefinitely — to recognize and kill leukemic cells if they ever return."

Dan was amazed at the biology involved and wondered if even Sue Sampson really understood it any better than he did.

Certainly, the biology was much more complicated than what he dealt with in solid organ transplantation. In bone marrow transplantation, the idea was to replace the recipient's immune system as completely as possible, partly in anticipation that the new immune system, derived from the donor, would forever prevent the re-emergence of leukemic cells. But in the year following Michael's original bone marrow transplant, Dan learned that it wasn't so simple. One of the first bone marrow biopsies performed after the transplant revealed that Michael's marrow was genetically *chimeric* — half of the bone marrow cells were his and half were Lauren's. One month later, a routine marrow biopsy showed that all of the cells were Lauren's. Was chimerism preferred to complete replacement with the donor's marrow? While complete replacement with donor cells might assure a more potent anti-leukemic effect, it also might increase the risk of GVHD. It was clear to Dan that even the experts did not completely understand the biology. *Perhaps someday our collective consciousness will understand all of this and more.*

"Fantastic stuff, Susan. Have you had any experience with this technique here at Children's?"

"Honestly — no. And we're going to need guidance from Seattle regarding the length of the cell culture and the dose of IL-2. I'll admit, this is cutting edge stuff but I'm recommending that we give it a shot. It's possible that it won't work at all — especially if we don't infuse enough of the T-cells. There's also a risk of serious GVHD if we overdose Michael with Lauren's cells."

Kathy had only loosely followed the discussion about lymphocytes and interleukins, but chimed in, "Let's do it."

One week later, the procedure was performed with no particular hoopla. Lauren was hoping for another bone marrow aspiration — actually for another dose of ketamine — but settled for the simpler peripheral blood donation (years later she would refer to it as "my heroic and painful phlebotomy"). Michael was feeling fine. Even before the T-cell infusions, his blood counts had returned close to normal. There were no infectious complications this time around. And there were no immediate adverse effects from the T-cell transfusion.

"So what now?" Kathy asked Sue Sampson during her morning rounds.

"I've asked Peds Surg to remove Michael's Broviac. He can be discharged by early afternoon."

"Discharged?" After the dreadful experience and prolonged hospitalization four years ago, this seemed all too easy.

"If the T-cell infusions are going to work, we really won't know for months or even years. In fact, there is no particular way to monitor the T-cells other than making sure that the remission is sustained. Michael will need a prescription for cyclosporine — we use relatively low doses to prevent graft versus host disease. He'll need monthly blood tests to monitor his counts and his cyclosporine blood levels. Otherwise, I suggest you take Michael home and lead all of your lives as normally as possible."

Fifteen

San Francisco —
July 1998

By the late spring, Michael was doing remarkably well and Dan felt obliged to arrange a celebratory family summer vacation. He realized that it may have been the last chance to take a vacation with all of the Ulek kids. Tom was in the middle of a five-year plan at Ohio State but once he graduated *(okay, if he graduated)* it was unlikely that he would be joining Mom and Dad for family fun time much longer. And Michael was doing well, but pessimist Dan worried about how long this latest remission would last. *Mr. Doom and Gloom.*

Kathy and Dan chose San Francisco for this family vacation. They had traveled there for the first time for their honeymoon.

Back then, they stayed at the Civic Center Holiday Inn, spent every penny of their wedding gift money, ate at unaffordable high-end restaurants, and returned home completely broke after having the time of their life — in more ways than one. Over the years, Dan traveled to San Francisco many times for meetings and talks, sometimes taking Kathy for extended trips. But none of the kids had ever been there — or for that matter, anywhere west of Chicago — so they knew this would be a special treat. Dan had accumulated more than 300,000 frequent flyer miles and was able to fly the entire family to San Francisco for free — paying for his own ticket, of course, so as to collect even more frequent flyer miles. It would be particularly nice for Dan because this was going be a *true* vacation — no talks, meetings, or other professional obligations.

Kathy and Dan had some concerns that San Francisco might not be kid-friendly. *Honey, did you know that 80 percent of males living in San Francisco are gay?* However, by the end of the vacation, they realized that their kids were growing up quickly, and that the experience on the West Coast was a good one for the entire family.

On the flight from Cleveland, Dan talked to his kids about Jack Kerouac, his classic book "On the Road" and the saga of modern America's West Coast culture. As a child of the sixties, he was very familiar with the San Francisco chronology: beatniks in North Beach, Allen Ginsberg and Neal Cassady, the City of Lights Bookstore, Owsley's acid, Electric Kool-Aid Acid Tests, Hell's Angels, the Grateful Dead, hippies in Haight-Ashbury, Fillmore West Auditorium, the summer of love, and George Harrison's unhappy visit to a Love-In in Golden Gate Park. Dan had never managed to attend a Grateful Dead concert, but he considered himself a Dead Head at heart — still having a collection of tie-dye T-shirts that he now brought out only for special occasions (basically never). If he hadn't met Kathy, he surely would have applied for residency or fellowship programs in San Francisco or in other California cities. In addition to recounting the history of the counterculture, Dan tried to prepare the kids for the extraordinary beauty of San Francisco and the Bay area: the Golden Gate Bridge, Sausalito, Napa Valley, the Presidio and marina, the trolley cars, and the spectacular views of the hilly city as seen from the intersection of Mason and Sacramento streets.

Their base camp was the Marriott at Fisherman's Wharf. Dan rented a van for travels around the area — *automatic* transmission. Highlights of the weeklong vacation included: lunch at Pebble Beach country club, a visit to the redwood forest at Muir Woods, a ride on the trolley cars from Fisherman's Wharf to Union Square, and a stroll through Haight Ashbury including photo shoots of the old Grateful Dead House on Ashbury and a stroll down Haight toward the east end of Golden Gate Park. "Dad, what's a head shop?"

Dan accidentally-on-purpose drove through the Castro District and was surprised that the twins knew, more or less, what *gay* meant. Kathy: "Oh my, that fellow's rear end is showing through the back of his trousers!" Lauren: "Mom, he's just gay." There were great family meals at the Fisherman's Wharf itself, in China Town, Pier 39, Sausalito, SoMa, and at the Cliff House – the restaurant/tourist attraction overlooking the Pacific Ocean and a herd of sea lions basking on wooden docks near the west end of Golden Gate Park.

On the second-last day of the vacation, Dan arranged for a salmon fishing excursion on one of the many charter boats harbored at Fisherman's Wharf. The boat would depart at 5:30 a.m., travel through the San Francisco bay, under the Golden Gate Bridge, and then about five miles into the Pacific Ocean west of the city. When he called for the reservations the day before, the boat's captain was less than enthusiastic about having children aboard. "There will be at least two other adult parties fishing on the same charter. If your kids get seasick, I can't turn back — you'll just have to deal with them. And remember, it's a six-hour excursion."

That night, he bought Dramamine patches for the entire family at a nearby drugstore. The kids wanted Italian food on their second last night, and the family feasted on meatballs and spaghetti at a southern Italian restaurant in Ghirardelli Square: rich red tomato sauce on traditional spaghetti and lots of buttery garlic bread. Dan and Kathy split a bottle of inky Chianti. Because Kathy kept her red wine consumption down to a single glass, Dan basically drank the entire bottle. Before heading back to the hotel, there was chocolate ice cream for all from an ice cream store in Ghirardelli Square.

Dan had spent a lot of time on boats in Lake Erie as a child and had never been seasick. There is always a first time for everything. While the bay was calm, the waters became choppy as the fishing boat — about a forty-footer — ventured beyond the Golden Gate Bridge. Soon they were mulling through five- to ten-foot waves in the ocean. One of the other parties on the boat was an older African American couple who brought aboard a cooler containing two six-packs of Bud Light and a bucket of Kentucky Fried Chicken. *It's six o'clock in the morning!*

As the captain slowed the boat down to give instructions for baiting the lines, Dan felt an unfamiliar queasiness that he was able to quell. That is, until the African American woman opened the bucket of chicken. One whiff and Dan experienced an eruption of nausea like he had never experienced before. Everyone else seemed to be fine. As all the passengers and crew were collected in the boat's aft to begin baiting their lines, Dan craftily headed to the front of the boat and heaved yesterday's spaghetti dinner into the ocean: spaghetti, meatballs, Chianti, and chocolate. After five minutes of heaving, he looked back and was happy to see that no one had noticed him hurling his guts out. Surely his stomach had been completely emptied and he would be fine for the rest of the excursion. Wrong. There was plenty of fried chicken in that bucket, and each time the black woman opened the bucket, Dan got another whiff and headed back to the front of the boat. Kathy spotted him on about his third trip and stifled a smile.

"Are you okay?"

"Kath, please don't tell the kids. They're having so much fun and I don't want to spoil it. And the captain won't turn back for my sake anyhow. I think I'll be fine now. I just wish I would have bought some Dramamine for myself. By the way, how many meatballs did I eat last night? I told you I wanted *northern* Italian food. Oh my God, they're opening the KFC bucket again!" Kathy personally counted eight trips to the front of the boat.

She successfully kept the kids distracted — and only years later would tell them the story about Kentucky Fried Chicken and their seasick Dad. The fishing trip ended *(Thank God!)* without the kids having any clue. As they boated through the calmer waters of the bay, past Alcatraz and toward Fisherman's Wharf, Dan was not too miserable to notice how much fun the day had been for Kathy and the kids. All totaled, they hauled in over sixty pounds of salmon. Michael was beaming, having caught four salmon himself, including the largest catch of the day. They planned to have the fish cleaned, filleted and frozen at the Wharf and shipped back home. Dan had not seen Michael this happy for many years. The entire family was happy. It was a good time that was well-deserved by a family that had been through some rough times.

As they taxied into Fisherman's Wharf, Dan noticed that Michael had some blisters around his eyes and that his lips were peeling. It had been partially sunny out in the ocean, but everyone in the family was wearing long-sleeved clothing and hats on the fishing excursion, anticipating cool temperatures and some ocean spray beyond the Golden Gate Bridge. Dan examined Michael's face more carefully without being obvious about his inspection. This was not sunburn. It was the early sign of graft versus host disease.

Sixteen

Valentine's Day — February 2001

Kathy and Nancy each drove separately to Four Birds, a new restaurant in Shaker Square featuring new California cuisine. Both of their husbands were going to arrive late and would be driving separately.

Kathy arrived first and sipped some ice water while eyeing the menu. Nancy arrived ten minutes later. She appeared flustered and walked in with a slight stagger. *Maybe a cocktail or two at home before dinner?* Over the last five years, she had gained some weight and was wearing a black pantsuit that did nothing to hide her midriff bulge. She was a bleached blonde when Kathy first met her almost twenty years ago. Gradually she let her hair transition to a darker color and she now wore it very short — almost a boyish style. She had a pretty face but never wore makeup of any kind. Kathy often thought she'd look more attractive with just a little lipstick.

"Sorry I'm late. Jack went to the OR in the late afternoon to deal with an urgent aortic dissection. He called me around five and said the case might take hours and not to plan on his coming to dinner."

Earlier, Dan called Kathy and said that he was just starting to write progress notes on twelve patients. He would try to make it, but might be there only for dessert and a glass of wine. "Dan's going to be late, too. Such is life these days."

Both wives agreed that academic medicine and surgery had taken a turn for the worse in their lifetimes. Their husbands could have made far more money working in private practice. In the old days, the allure of academia was the chance to teach and to do research — all with the expectation that time would be protected for these activities. In recent years, protected time seemed to be nonexistent. Teaching, and especially research, increasingly required extended work hours because the main part of each day was devoted to patient care with few exceptions. These Valentine's Day dinners were great fun in the early Ulek-Hurtuk years. After nights like this, Kathy and Nancy wondered if the tradition was worth preserving.

They ordered a bottle of Sauvignon Blanc and lied to the waiter, telling him that they were expecting their husbands momentarily. As had become customary, they updated each other on the status of their children and other family members. Both of the Hurtuk kids were now on living on the West Coast. Steven had landed a job with a software company in San Francisco. Susan was at Stanford and had a *serious* boyfriend. Kathy returned the volley with an update on her four children — and yes, Michael was still in remission.

After her second glass of wine, Nancy opened the evening's main discussion.

"Has Dan talked to you about the Pittsburgh position?"

At that point, Kathy was aware that some special leadership position was open in Pittsburgh and that both Dan and Jack might be considered candidates, but she was lacking details.

"Not so much. But I think he is going to Pittsburgh later this month to give a talk and maybe have an informal interview. But I don't think he's seriously interested. To be honest, Dan's had lots of job offers in the past five years, but I think he's happy at CMC."

"Wish I could say the same for Jack. He's been going through a protracted mid-life crisis for ten years now. He really wants to be a department chair, but right now it looks like Schick will never step down at CMC. He says he wants the Pittsburgh job, but honestly I think it's the last thing he needs — more responsibilities and stresses in the front lines. I think Jack needs a job where he can cut back on operating and patient care — that's what stresses him out. Besides — you're not gonna believe it — I actually like Cleveland and really don't want to move to Pittsburgh. I mean, really — the Steelers?"

This marked the first time that Nancy and Kathy ever discussed the Pittsburgh job. In fact, after almost fifteen years of regular dinners, it was the first time they ever had any meaningful discussion at all — more often, they were the soft-spoken wives coming to these dinners as the submissive spouses of their dominant doctor husbands. Once the conversations turned to medical business, the wives knew that the evening was winding down. It was a nice change of pace to chat without the men there.

Dan called Kathy on her cell phone to say that he wasn't going to make it. One of the new heart transplant patients just had a cardiac arrest and he would be there for several more hours getting him stabilized in the CICU.

Nancy summoned their waiter. "Can we get another bottle of this Sauvignon? We're not quite ready to order," she remarked, beginning to feel relaxed.

"You know, Kathy, I've always admired you for being so — normal. Let me ask you a question: Has Dan ever cheated on you?"

As far as she knew, aside from some high school dating before they met at Loyola, Kathy and Dan had a monogamous relationship since their early twenties. "I don't think so. Why, do you think Jack has?"

"Twice that I know about. First time, I almost filed for divorce, but he made up and promised to be better. Second time, I think was a one-night stand. To me, it's all part of his macho, power hungry, rising-to-the-top personality."

Kathy did recall Jack's comment a few years back — again after a few generous drinks — "All men cheat. It's just what they do."

Nancy went on, "Don't get me wrong; I still love him — I always will. I just wish sometimes I could get him off his power trip — best job, best house, best kids, top colleges. I wish we could just settle back and be normal — more like you and Dan."

Kathy nodded to accept the compliment, but wondered whether she and Dan weren't more like Nancy and Jack than it appeared. Compared to the mammoth Hurtuk home in Shaker Heights, Kathy and Dan's home in Solon was modest: 2.800-square-foot colonial with four needed bedrooms. But Dan was always talking about moving to a bigger house — maybe something on Lake Erie with our own in-ground pool. From Kathy's point of view, she had great children — none of them ever got into any serious trouble — but the reality is they were all, at best, average to above-average students. Tom went to Ohio State. She would be delighted if Michael got into any college after dealing with his illness, and it was still too early to tell with the twins who were basically getting *A*'s and *B*'s early in high school. Dan was always thinking Ivy League. In his own way, Dan was just as power hungry as Jack, and Kathy was just beginning to sense that competition for this Pittsburgh position was fueling his burning need to be a winner. She now even wondered if tonight's emergencies at CMC weren't subconsciously crafted to avoid a get-together. And maybe Dan *has* been cheating — God knows he has had plenty of opportunities with all the traveling he does on his own.

Kathy paused, stared at her wine glass, and realized that she was getting drunk.

"Nancy, time for me to back off on the wine if I ever want to drive home. Maybe we should order some food?"

"I'm actually not that hungry," responded Nancy. How does coffee and dessert sound to you? To be honest, I really enjoyed our little outing without the husbands. Let's do it more often."

Kathy drove home thinking. She loved her life and she loved Dan. Of course, he doesn't cheat — that was the wine talking. But after all these years of marriage, did she really know her husband? Did she really understand his ambitions? Was he driven by demons that she didn't comprehend? Was he anxious to move up the ladder or just escaping from some insecurity of the past and present?

God, I hope he doesn't really want to move to Pittsburgh.

Seventeen

New York City —
May 2001

Kathy and Dan both loved New York. Dan would get invited
to the city at least once or twice a year for meetings or invited
talks and, when Kathy could join him, always added a day or two
to relax, eat at great restaurants, and see some Broadway shows.
This time, he was invited to give what had recently become his
standard talk, "Prevention of chronic cardiac transplant rejection: the role of immune monitoring tests," at a symposium organized by the transplant center at Columbia-Presbyterian Medical
Center. The symposium was held at the Marriott Marquis Hotel,
in the heart of Times Square and within a short walking distance
of all the major Broadway theaters. Dan's talk was on Friday

afternoon. After his session, the remainder of the symposium was devoted mostly to kidney and liver transplantation, and not to heart transplantation, so he did not feel obligated to stay for the other lectures. It was a perfect opportunity to spend a long weekend in Manhattan.

On Saturday morning, he and Kathy took a taxi to Little Italy, had an early lunch at one of the many Italian cafes lining Mulberry Street, then wandered up and down Canal Street and stocked up on cheap replica colognes, two-dollar neckties, and fake watches. For years, the kids thought that Mom and Dad traveled to New York to buy expensive watches for them as Christmas or birthday gifts. When they brought Tom to New York a year earlier, the cat was out of the bag. "Dad, these watches all cost five bucks!" It was true. During his entire professional life, Dan had never worn any watch other than those that he had purchased for ten bucks or less on Canal Street. *I love New York!*

They returned to the Marquis, had late afternoon cocktails in the eighth floor bar overlooking Seventh Avenue, and then went back to their room for some planned lovemaking before going to the theater. *Hurtuk was right — eating, screwing, and getting intoxicated — it was fun to do all three in different places.*

In recent years, Dan and Kathy had many discussions about planned versus spontaneous sex. Spontaneous sex was great, and in the early years of their marriage it was the norm — each of them initiating it with about equal frequency — and often in venues other than the master bedroom at home. In recent years, the spontaneity had declined considerably. Busy schedules and four kids in the house were the usual excuses. In addition, Kathy went through an early menopause and admitted that her libido was not what it used to be. Planned sex had become their routine now and traveling and staying in hotels provided good opportunities. Kathy would have a glass of wine while taking a hot bubble bath and then would join Dan naked in bed. They had gone through the same pleasant routine the day before. Dan could not remember the last time that he and Kathy had sex twice in two days at home. And today she had two orgasms — much like the early days after they were married. Later, they went to see *Phantom of the Opera.* As they prepared for bed, they both agreed that this truly had been a romantic weekend. *We should travel more often!*

Their return flight Sunday was scheduled for 3 p.m., so they had time for brunch. It was a beautiful spring morning in the city and Dan suggested a walk down Seventh Avenue to one of his favorite restaurants overlooking Bryant Park. The birch trees were in full bloom and the park was already filled with roller bladers, joggers, and local folks on park benches sipping lattes or cappuccinos and reading the Sunday New York Times. Kathy and Dan rarely ate breakfast at home, but a big breakfast or brunch had become a last-day-of-trip tradition for them over the years when they traveled. They each ordered screwdrivers and eggs Benedict.

In their window seat, the late morning sun was shining on Kathy's face and Dan once again thought to himself that Kathy had become more and more attractive with age. In contrast, Dan felt that he was aging poorly. He inherited his father's male-pattern baldness, started losing his hair after the age of thirty, and now had little hair on the top of his head with rapidly graying sideburns. He had struggled to control his weight for several years, recently upgrading to trousers with a thirty-eight-inch waist. *If I reach forty inches, I will officially have "metabolic syndrome."* At 5 feet 10 inches and 205 pounds, his body mass index was 29.4 — *overweight* and bordering on the official definition of *obese. One large meal or a day of constipation and there I am: obese.* Especially because he mostly took care of patients with heart disease, Dan could not tolerate the idea of his patients, family, or friends knowing that he had his own risk factors for cardiovascular disease. He already had a strong family history of heart problems. Both his grandfather and a paternal uncle dropped dead of heart attacks in their late fifties. His father died of heart failure complicated by lithium-induced renal disease that necessitated dialysis for six months before his death.

Dan was a closet smoker for years but quit cold turkey just before his fortieth birthday. He kept his blood pressure under control, so long as he remembered to take his self-prescribed angiotensin converting enzyme inhibitor combined with a low dose of hydrochlorothiazide. Keeping his weight down was one of his biggest challenges.

Kathy, on the other hand, had started exercising routinely in recent years and was more fit than ever. She joined an exercise club in Solon and was speed-walking between seven and eight miles at a time, three or four days a week. She befriended some fellow power walkers and enjoyed chatting and walking with them. Dan and Tom routinely kidded her about her walking boy-friends. "They are all men in their seventies for goodness sake!" Kathy would say. *Yea, but bet they still have fantasies about getting into your pants.* Kathy once weighed 145 pounds, but at 5 feet 8 inches still looked good. Now she was down to 125 pounds and looked sexier than ever — a thin waistline accentu-ating her feminine hips, and breasts still perky for a woman who just turned fifty-one. She was wearing her brown hair shorter and Dan liked the look.

"What's the matter, Dan? You look distracted."

He indeed had some things on his mind other than his wife's figure. "I checked my e-mail this morning while you were in the shower. Jack Hurtuk e-mailed me to let me know we are being sued — a pleasant little way to end our romantic weekend in New York."

"Who is suing you?"

Dan had not mentioned anything about this case to Kathy previously. Over the years, he had been named in four other malpractice lawsuits — each of which he felt was frivolous — and ultimately dropped without any jury trials or settlements. Although those cases were "frivolous," they each invoked fear and loathing for the justice system and feelings of guilt — not to mention many sleepless nights worrying about an award that would exceed the malpractice cap. Under those circumstances, the prosecutors could go after personal assets — your savings, property — everything you own. In reality, this rarely happened, but it still entered every doctor's mind whenever they received one of those green-striped certified letters with a subpoena or what lawyers called a *ninety day notice*: "Dear Dr. So-and-So: This letter is being sent to inform you that we are contemplating a lawsuit regarding this-and-that and so-and-so. We will make our decision in ninety days." *Thanks, and I hope you sleep well for the next three months, too.*

Apparently, Hurtuk received his green-striped letter Friday. It was not a ninety day notice — it was the real deal. The suit named the hospital, Ulek, Hurtuk, and Marilyn Banks, one of the heart transplant coordinators, and claimed that they were responsible for a wrongful death.

In his e-mail, Hurtuk said, "I'm really upset about this, Dan. I did the transplant a year before the medical mistake happened and really wasn't following the patient at the time. That's why we have the medical team — to provide proper long-term care of our patients. I am only being named because I am the overall program director. I talked to Bill Matthews from legal and he is concerned that this one will go to court. Anyhow, enjoy your vacation. Talk more about it tomorrow."

That last part about a "vacation" was a not-so-subtle jab. In fact, Dan was taking no vacation time but simply spending an off-weekend with Kathy after giving an invited talk on Friday. From his perspective, invited talks constituted work, not vacation. He had been on-call the weekend before and would be on-call again next weekend, but it didn't seem to register with Hurtuk. Both privately and publicly, Hurtuk would refer to his travels as "vacations." Dan was increasingly convinced that Hurtuk was trying to portray him as an academic researcher whose travel posed a detriment to patient care. He secretly wondered if he had discussed this during his interviews in Pittsburgh. They rarely if ever discussed the nature of their separate interviews at Pittsburgh. Clearly, the competition for the position in Pittsburgh was creating friction in a professional relationship that had previously been amicable and productive. At least Dan had no further travel plans until the first week of September. It was going to be a busy summer on the inpatient service.

"I'm sorry, Kathy. What did you say?"

"Wow, you really *are* distracted. I asked who is suing you."

"I didn't want to bring this up because I presumed it would turn out to be another frivolous case that would be dropped. I didn't think that both of us needed to worry about it."

"Dan, you should know me better than that."

"Well, I was actually deposed a couple of months ago and came away with the feeling that the case would be dropped. But Jack thinks the case will go to a jury trial because it revolves around a medical mistake, and that's a term that lights up the eyes of prosecuting attorneys."

"So what was the medical mistake?"

"The patient was Samuel Bennings — a young man in his forties when he got transplanted for idiopathic cardiomyopathy a couple of years ago. The surgery all went very smoothly. He was out of the hospital in less than three weeks. The kicker is that he was a Medicaid patient, so essentially we saved his life for almost no compensation. Hell, I'm not even sure if I ever collected a penny for any of my services. On top of that, he turned out to be grossly noncompliant. He had two early rejection episodes in the first month after his initial hospital discharge from not taking his immunosuppressants properly — and expense wasn't the issue because he had Medicaid coverage.

Anyhow, about eight months after the transplant, he called Marilyn Banks asking for prescription refills. He was in a research study and was taking cyclosporine and sirolimus as his main anti-rejection drugs. Marilyn called in the prescriptions to the guy's pharmacy, including sirolimus 5 mg per day. Months later, it became clear that the prescription was written for *tacrolimus*, not *sirolimus*."

"Was that bad?" Kathy asked.

"Well, the names sound similar but the two drugs work differently. Tacrolimus is a cousin of cyclosporine, so he was essentially taking two drugs in the same class. The problem is that these drugs are both nephrotoxic — they can cause both acute and chronic kidney damage. The patient missed all of his office appointments for about four months and then showed up in the ER vomiting. Blood tests showed that he had severe kidney failure and he had to start dialysis. Only when the family brought in his bag of medications was the mistake realized. He later developed sepsis related to an infected dialysis catheter and died."

"So how is any of that your fault?"

"It was clearly a medical mistake. The problem is that the prosecuting lawyers really don't know who to blame. Marilyn swears she called in sirolimus. The pharmacist claims otherwise. Of course Marilyn must call in prescriptions under the name of a physician — in this case, me. Ultimately, I am responsible."

"That sounds crazy. And why was Hurtuk named?"

"Oh, he's pissed about that — probably because he's the program director. In general, they tend to name lots of people initially, and then whittle it down to just a few parties — usually the hospital and the docs because they have the biggest insurance policies. I'm guessing that's why they didn't go after the pharmacist. To this day, I have no idea which pharmacist took the call."

"Honey, are you really worried about this? It seems like you and Jack did nothing wrong."

Although Dan had never been named in a lawsuit that ended up as a court case or with an out-of-court settlement, he had served as an expert witness in three medical malpractice jury trials during his career. "Kath, getting to court is every prosecutor's dream. When the jury sees the family sobbing in the back of the courtroom as they relive their loved one's painful injury or death, the facts of the case become irrelevant. The prevailing mood is that *someone* should compensate the grief-stricken family. Some system of justice, huh?"

"So when will you know if this case is going to court?"

"It's all up to a judge. Jack said the legal department doesn't expect to hear anything until the fall. Just one more thing to worry about this summer."

Dan was sorry that he had two screwdrivers with brunch — now feeling somewhere between pleasantly relaxed and overtly tired. "Hey, let's take a cab to St. Patrick's. We can be back at the hotel by noon in time to pick up our bags and head to LaGuardia."

Since 1994, it had become another Ulek tradition that whenever they were in Manhattan, they would make a side trip to St. Patrick's Cathedral on Fifth Avenue. The massive interior of the church with its gothic arches and lofty ceilings created an eerie oasis in the heart of bustling mid-town Manhattan. If they had time and Mass was being said, they would stay for at least part of it. With or without the Mass, they would visit the statue of Saint Peregrine Laziosi, the patron saint of patients suffering from cancer, throw a dollar or two in the gift box and light two candles for Michael. More often than not, Dan was alone in the city for a meeting or a talk and surprised himself by faithfully fulfilling the tradition. Each time, he would find himself in a short-lived state of meditation, catching a fleeting glimpse of some reality that he could not pin down. *Some collective wisdom — maybe God — was it — nirvana? Why was the aura always so transient and mysterious?* While Dan's devotion to the Catholic Church had flagged, he still made the trip to St. Patrick's during every trip to New York, lighting the candles for Michael and hoping to extend that glimpse.

While sitting through the offertory of the Sunday Mass with Kathy, Dan looked upward to the stained glass windows, closed his eyes and once again began to get that feeling — of some greater presence. "Dan, let's go; we need to get back to the Marquis if we're going to get our luggage and make our flight," said Kathy. The glimpse faded and the feeling was gone.

Eighteen

Cleveland Medical Center — Early August 2001

Dan arranged a meeting with Rick Weichel to openly discuss the Pittsburgh situation, wanting to make sure that he was completely apprised of the possibilities, including the possibility that he might accept the position and leave the CMC. He was not surprised to learn that Weichel was already aware that he was looking at the position at the Pittsburgh State Institute.

"Listen, Dan, this is actually a great thing and I appreciate your coming to discuss it. I have mixed feelings, of course, but every academic medical center should take pride in developing faculty who move on to bigger and better things. So what's the story? Do you think you have the edge over Hurtuk?"

"Jack and I are good friends but it's been awkward for us to discuss this whole thing. In fact, it's made for a stressful summer. I've been on service all summer and we've been doing five transplants a month — so it's been very busy and we have had few opportunities to talk, either professionally or socially. I know that each of us has already had three interviews in Pittsburgh and mine have gone well. They have invited me for a fourth interview after the international meeting in September and asked for Kathy to join me — you know, to look at real estate. I take that as a good sign. By the way, did you know I was invited to give the keynote address at the Paris meeting?"

Dan decided not to tell Weichel that Tom Stallings from the Pittsburgh Transplant Institute might be meeting with him in Paris. Secretly, he hoped that Stallings might make a job offer right there in Paris.

Weichel himself was an invasive cardiologist who specialized in electrophysiology — performing lucrative ablation procedures on patients with arrhythmias. He was an international expert on atrial arrhythmias, especially paroxysmal atrial tachycardias. He had no interest or expertise in heart transplantation, so essentially lived in a different academic world than Dan, aside from serving as his Division Chief.

"Yes, I've seen the brochures — looks like a nice program and Paris will not be too shabby. Congratulations on the keynote address; it's another feather in your cap, and I suspect that the Pittsburgh Institute will be impressed. By the way, what's going on with your NIH renewal?"

Dan's mood flipped. He wasn't expecting Weichel to bring this up. Earlier in the week, he received the score for the renewal of his NIH RO1 grant. RO1 grants were the most coveted of the investigator-initiated research grants sponsored by the National Institutes of Health. The most successful research scientists in the medical field often had two or even three RO1s. Dan had just one, but many young investigators in the medical field never succeeded in landing even a single RO1 and were forced out of research-based careers. Moreover, Dan had successfully renewed the grant for three cycles — each for a five year period. The score on his re-search proposal seeking funding for a fourth cycle was 155. Theo-retically, that was on a scale of 100 to 500 with 100 being best, but in the modern era, grants with scores higher than 300 were "triaged," i.e., they were dismissed after only a cursory review and not scrutinized further. For his first three NIH grants, he had scores between 125 and 150. For the current year, he figured that his score of 155 would rank in the top 15 to 20 percent of submit-ted grants. But the difference between the 15th and 20th percentile was critical. NIH funds were extremely limited and the cutoff for funding currently was closer to the 15th percentile. In other words, his chances of getting re-funded were marginal — ultimately the decision was up to the NIH, depending almost entirely on their budget for the current year.

For Dan, re-funding from the NIH was essential. During the past seven years, he had reduced his dependency on clinical RVUs by supporting his salary from other sources — mostly a hospital stipend for serving as Medical Director of Heart Trans-plantation and a number of smaller research grants, including a mid-career development award from the American Heart As-sociation. If his RO1 was not renewed, he would be back at the table with Weichel talking about reduced travel or increased clinical service. More importantly, Dan did not want to go into his fourth interview at Pittsburgh without renewed NIH funding. *Hurtuk has never had NIH funding. He's a great surgeon but he has never had an RO1. Surely Pittsburgh must be aware . . .*

"Timely question, Rick. I just got the score on the RO1 re-newal — 155. I haven't received the pink sheets from the NIH reviewers yet. I think it's good enough for funding."

"Hmmm — going to be close, Dan."

Rounds the next morning were painful. Hurtuk was in a foul mood and as usual, decided to take it out on the resident staff. The team was rounding on Martha Ulesky, now out seven days from her heart transplant and just transferred yesterday from the CICU to a regular telemetry floor in the Tower. She had been maintained on a ventricular-assist device for three months before receiving her transplant. These devices were life-savers, but most patients exposed to the apparatus developed antibodies that cross-reacted with human tissues, thus markedly increasing the risk of early rejection. Rejection could be treated and usually reversed with intensification of the patient's immunosuppression, but severe cases of rejection could lead to cardiac dysfunction that could result in transient heart failure or even death.

Hurtuk was at the bedside routinely scanning the flow sheet depicting Martha's vital signs, her list of medications and their doses, and laboratory results — all displayed serially since the day of transplantation.

"Yesterday's tacrolimus level was only 3 ng/ml."

He leaned over to the chief resident who suddenly looked petrified. "Dr. Anthony, was her dose adjusted upward last night?"

"Umm — Dr. Hurtuk, I think the intern called the cardiology fellow to adjust the dose."

Dan knew that Don Anthony was in big trouble. There was no cardiology fellow rotating on the inpatient transplant service this month. When Hurtuk organized the service years ago, he reluctantly agreed to allow the cardiology service to manage immunosuppression on the transplant recipients. He knew that he was perfectly capable of adjusting immunosuppressive drug doses, but in the interest of maintaining an interdisciplinary service, he acquiesced and gave that job to his medical colleagues. In the normal daily routine, one of the surgical residents was responsible for calling the cardiology service with all of the immunosuppressive drug levels that were usually reported by the laboratory in the early evening. When there was a cardiology fellow on the service, Dan allowed the fellow to take these calls with the understanding that he was available for backup when needed. Dan suddenly realized that he did not get a call about drug levels the night before. Under those circumstances, he presumed that all the levels were in the therapeutic range. Martha's level was 3 when it should have been somewhere between 8 and 15.

"You *think*?" Hurtuk asked, raising his voice. "Would you like to *think* again? Maybe you would like to *think* about whether you want to finish your residency here! There is no *goddamn* cardiology fellow assigned to this service for the month of August." Now he was screaming. "So I want to know: *Who* was called? Was it *me*? God knows I sleep with my phone and beeper next to my head every day of my life, and — *no* — I do not recall getting a call about a *goddamn* tacrolimus level of 3 on a fresh transplant patient."

Dan closed his eyes and wished that Hurtuk would lower his voice. These little demonstrations of power and authority always occurred within earshot of the patients. He could just see Martha on the other side of the door thinking, *Oh my Lord, my tacrolimus level is subtherapeutic and I am going to die! These doctors have no idea what they are doing!* It's amazing that behavior like this didn't precipitate more lawsuits — or maybe there were more suits against Hurtuk that Dan didn't know about.

"I hope you realize, Dr. Anthony, that we are managing Mrs. Ulesky with a unique steroid-free protocol. More so than with other protocols, it is absolutely essential to maintain therapeutic tacro levels with this protocol. So I ask again, who was called to adjust this level? *Me? No!* The cardiology fellow? *Hell no!* Maybe Dr. Ulek? — or was he on *vacation*?"

Bastard.

Hurtuk continued his rage. "No — I don't believe *anyone* was called. Let us all just hope to hell that Mrs. Ulesky doesn't have a rejection episode based on your collective laziness and stupidity."

Although the residents, especially Don Anthony, were visibly shaken, Dan knew that much of Hurtuk's anger was directed at him, not the residents. Was it just the usual tension between a surgeon and an internist, or had this competition for the Pittsburgh job strained the foundation of the service that Hurtuk and Ulek had proudly organized many years ago?

After rounds, Dan walked back toward his office with Hurtuk after dismissing the other members of the rounding team.

"I'll take the blame for missing that tacrolimus level, Jack. It's early in the academic year and I don't think the new surgical interns are familiar with the routine. I should have called in last night to check on the levels."

"Just seems that things have gotten kind of sloppy lately. But no, the blame for that is mine — after all, I am the overall director. The service has been busy but I've also been preoccupied by the Pittsburgh position. I'm thinking that maybe the time is right for a career change. I'm not getting any younger, Dan. By the way, is your application there still active?"

Dan was perplexed by the question, which once again implied that a non-surgeon had no business applying for a leadership position of this magnitude. Of course his application was active. Perhaps Jack was not aware that he had been invited for a fourth interview, together with his wife.

"As far as I know," said Dan, stretching the truth. "Have you been invited back for another interview, Jack?"

"Not yet. I was told they would make that decision after the international meeting in Paris."

Aha, I have the upper hand! But I will not let on. When Jack got upset, Dan's approach usually was to flatter him — that tended to cool him off quickly. "Well, I'm sure you will get invited for another interview in the fall, Jack. Word on the street is that you are the top candidate."

That night, he recounted the day's events with Kathy. "You'd better be careful that you don't alienate Jack too much," she said. "He's been a good friend. In fact, he's one of the only friends you've got."

It wasn't the first time that Kathy had mentioned his paucity of friends. In reality, Dan had no real friends other than his wife. He had professional acquaintances like Hurtuk and other physicians, and social acquaintances with a few neighbors, but no true friends that he could talk to openly — no one with whom he could share dreams, secrets, and fears. He didn't talk much to his family members either, save for his mother, their resident babysitter. But even with Mom, conversations were usually superficial. He had three older sisters and a younger brother and rarely talked with any of them, except during holiday get-togethers. As far as Dan was concerned, it was just the way he was raised. He honestly did not feel badly about his lack of friends, and seeing his siblings two or three times a year was plenty from his point of view.

Kathy, on the other hand, believed that friends became more important as one got older, and secretly worried that Dan would drive her crazy if he ever retired and had no friends other than her. She maintained close contact with at least a dozen old school friends, talked to each of them on a regular basis, and insisted on attending "girls night out" at least once every few months. When her mother was alive, she called her virtually every day and visited her several times each month. Five years after her mother died, her father retired from his factory job, got remarried and moved to southern Florida, but Kathy continued to talk to him by phone once a week.

"Well, you know Kath, one way or another, my friendship with Jack will likely end soon if either one of us is chosen for the Pittsburgh directorship. And right now it looks like we are the top two candidates."

As Dan thought about it, the only scenario that would be worse than personally being turned down for the job at Pittsburgh State would be for Hurtuk to be named to the position. Not only would Dan be devastated by the turndown, but he would be left in a heart transplant program with no senior surgical leadership. It could take years to replace Hurtuk with someone of comparable stature, and the program would likely lose some its national luster. All of this could ultimately influence his own research productivity, the quantity and quality of his publications, and his national and international reputation. Dan now realized that landing the Pittsburgh job was essential to continuing his successful career. He really needed to dazzle Tom Stallings if he got a chance to meet him at the September meeting in Paris.

Kathy winced a little, as she had not yet brought herself to telling Dan how unexcited she was about moving to Pittsburgh.

"Listen, Dan, you've really seemed stressed for the past two months — being on service for the whole summer and worrying about the Pittsburgh job at the same time — you need some down time, some time to relax. I've never seen you look so tired." She didn't want to bring up the *d* word (depression), because she already knew how he'd react. But she was worried about more than just Dan's fatigue *(Who wouldn't be tired when you are up almost every night for three consecutive months answering phone calls?)* — he seemed a little irritable at times and his concentration also seemed less sharp than usual. More importantly, their sex life had come close to a grinding halt for the summer. In the past, Dan was *never* too tired for sex. She knew that loss of libido was a sure sign of depression.

"Kath — five transplants a month for the past three months — that's stress. My stretch of on-service time is coming to an end soon. I'll have some down time after the meeting in Paris. I'm just overworked right now. I'll be fine."

Kathy's plan was for Dan to get a complete physical examination. Then, while he was in Paris, she intended to call Dan's new internist and inquire about treatment with an antidepressant.

Nineteen

Cleveland Medical Center —
Late August 2001

It was the last week of August and Dan had been attending on the inpatient transplant service for almost three consecutive months. During stretches like this, he needed to focus on patient care and his research studies and preparation for upcoming talks took a back seat. He was anxious to get through this long period of clinical service. While 90 percent of outcomes after heart transplantation were good ones, there were always complications, sometimes serious infections, and life-and-death issues that made these long stretches of clinical service stressful. Patient care itself — making diagnoses, prescribing therapies, discussing prognoses — was something at which Dan always excelled and once enjoyed.

However, over the years, there were increasing demands to provide written documentation of services rendered, to deal with case managers and insurance companies, to answer to quality assurance committees, to deal with litigious families, and of course, to deal with department chairmen and hospital administrators who were always demanding more productivity without provision of additional resources. Not to mention the recurring problem of patients with no insurance, lost insurance, or insurance inadequate to cover their medical expenses. There was nothing more disheartening than dealing with patients who experienced rejection, heart failure, and death because they could not afford their anti-rejection medications. Dan realized that, over time, his interest in patient care was waning and being replaced by interests in research, teaching, and travel — but he refused to admit it openly. He still wanted to maintain his reputation as an outstanding clinician.

The last thing Dan needed this morning was to find Jack Hurtuk in a teaching mood. *He must have no cases scheduled in the OR. We've got fifteen inpatients. We'll be rounding till noon.* On a typical morning, rounds on the inpatient service were conducted by two attendings (a surgeon and a cardiologist), as many as four residents, the inpatient nurse-coordinator, a pharmacist, a dietician, and sometimes medical students and other visitors. It was like a train of characters in white coats moving from room to room and from floor to floor, sometimes colliding with other trains, consisting of other subspecialty teams.

Teaching was an essential component of retaining an academic title, and teaching on rounds — sometimes called "bedside" teaching — was considered just as important as giving lectures in a medical school auditorium. When Dan was on service with Hurtuk, the teaching often took on an element of one-upmanship. Hurtuk would make a teaching point, for example about management of cardiac rejection. Dan would then quote the latest paper refuting or refining the comment, and Hurtuk would provide a rebuttal. All of this served to make rounds a bit theatrical as well as lengthy, but Ulek and Hurtuk were regularly ranked by residents as outstanding teachers, so the technique seemed to serve a purpose.

As Dan predicted, rounds ended just after 11:30 a.m. As they were finishing up decisions on the last patient in the CICU, Hurtuk pulled Dan aside for a word.

"Bet you're happy to be going off service. You look really tired, Dan."

"Actually I volunteered to cover through mid-September except for a meeting in New York and the Paris meeting — I asked Jack Friedewald to cover while I'm at those meetings. I'll be sure to give him a detailed sign-out."

It was clear that Hurtuk had no interest in sign-outs or who was covering what or when.

"I just learned yesterday that I've been dropped from the Bennings case. That's a relief."

"You mean the whole case has been dropped?"

"Not sure about that. I just got a certified letter from Bill Matthews telling me that I'm off the suit."

Not sure? I bet.

He returned to his office and had his secretary, Norma, call Matthews.

"Hi Bill. Has the Bennings case been dropped?"

"No, I'm afraid not. In fact, the plaintiff attorney is getting uglier and is refusing to settle more than ever. I think this one will go to jury trial as early as October, maybe even late September. The judge is sympathetic — you know, an indigent young African American patient dying from a medical mistake. He has this one high on his priority list."

"You're kidding . . . Hurtuk just told me he was dropped."

"Yes, but we all expected that. He wasn't really involved in the patient's care at the time of the medical mistake — I'm sorry, the *alleged* medical mistake. So at this point, it's just you and the hospital being named."

Shit. What about Marilyn Banks? What about the pharmacist?

"When will you know for sure about going to court?"

"We should know in the next two weeks. If it happens — I'll let you know as soon as possible so you can clear your calendar — probably for ten to fourteen days. With jury selection and all of the other preliminary stuff, these trials can take up to two weeks and it's hard to predict when they will call you in. You'll need to be available to the court on short notice."

Dan clicked on the Outlook calendar on his desktop computer. Following the New York and Paris meetings, he had talks, meetings, or visiting professorships scheduled in San Diego, Dallas, Barcelona (Kathy was planning to come), Boston, and Mexico City — all in a period of six weeks. In his entire career, he had never cancelled an invited talk or a visiting professorship, save for the two months after Michael was first diagnosed with AML. He could recall two occasions when talks or meetings were cancelled for circumstances beyond his control. He once missed a transplant meeting on Hawaii's Big Island because of a blizzard in Cleveland that shut down Hopkins Airport for two days. Two days later, Kathy's mother passed away from complications of her ovarian cancer. On another occasion, an evening dinner talk in Chicago was cancelled because mechanical problems on his outgoing plane delayed the flight, making it impossible to make the meeting on time. That evening, his son Tom fractured his fibula in a night-time skiing accident in upstate New York, and Dan ended up driving through the night to bring his son home. So when it came to talks and meetings, the word "cancellation" seemed to be a bad omen.

If the Bennings case went to court, he might have to cancel some or all of his upcoming talks at the last minute. *Maybe I should cancel them all now. But there goes the international recognition. There go my first class seats. There go the honoraria.* He didn't relish the idea of calling his meeting hosts to tell them that he was cancelling talks because he was defending himself against charges of malpractice and a wrongful death in front of a jury. More importantly, he constantly worried about going to court and losing the case. Would the prosecutors seek more than his insurance cap as an award? Would they go after his personal assets? Would his life be ruined?

Norma buzzed into his office to let him know that Kathy was on the phone.

"Hey. We're almost out of Tylenol. Can you pick up some before heading home today? Brian has a fever and I kept him home from school."

"Is he sick?"

"Just fever and fatigue, I'm sure it's that twenty-four hour flu going around."

Dan was about to tell Kathy about the Bennings case and his other woes, but he didn't have the energy. "Okay, see you tonight — make sure Brian drinks plenty of liquids."

Norma walked into Dan's office to deliver his mail and messages and found him with his head in his hands on the desk, sleeping.

Twenty

Paris —
September 11, 2001

The flight from Newark arrived in Paris forty minutes early thanks to a strong tailwind. Dan was thankful for the extra time to check into his hotel, immediately order a small pot of coffee from room service, take a wake-up shower, and then take one last look at his slides before heading to the conference. Although he drank almost no alcohol and slept for almost four hours on the plane, he felt unusually tired and struggled to stay awake. As he was unpacking, he remembered that he had grabbed his mail from his secretary the day before and stuffed it in his briefcase. As he was drying off from his shower, he poured himself some black coffee and went through his mail.

Amid lots of laboratory reports and throw-away advertisements from drug companies, he found a letter from National Institute for Allergy and Infectious Disease, the division of the NIH that was responsible for his RO1 renewal.

"Dear Dr Ulek:

Congratulations on the excellent score awarded to your recent renewal for grant RO1-3997645. This score ranked in the 18th percentile of grants submitted to your study section. Unfortunately, the score did not meet current thresholds for funding. We hope that you will revise your grant according to recommendations of the reviewers and consider re-submission in the next funding cycle. Thank you for submitting this proposal for renewed funding.

Sincerely,
Nancy Barton MD, PhD
NIAID"

Dan's mood sank. He wished he had waited to open his mail *after* his keynote address. *If I meet Tom Stallings, I'll pretend like I never saw this letter. Goddamnit.* He pulled out his laptop for one last review of his slides. *One last review.*

He quickly got into his best pinstripe suit — the old Marks and Spencer's beauty that he acquired in Hong Kong eight years earlier. He brought only a single necktie that Kathy had picked out for him — she knew all too well that Dan was notorious for mismatching his ties and shirts. He popped two memory sticks into his left pocket (an original and a back-up just in case) and his own laser pointer in his right pocket (never know when the battery will die on the pointer provided at the podium). The convention center was about a mile from his hotel — normally a twenty minute walk, but Dan's hotel was next to a Metro station and he thought he could save time by jumping on the subway. He forgot that he was taking the subway at the height of morning rush hour in Paris.

The train was packed shoulder to shoulder with commuters *(still some Europeans who don't believe in deodorant)*, but he made it to the convention center in plenty of time.

Registrations for this year's International Society of Heart Transplantation meeting were expected to exceed twenty-five hundred — the highest attendance in the history of the meeting. This international meeting was held every other year in different venues — mostly in some the world's nicest capitals. The meeting consisted largely of simultaneous sessions of abstract presentations appealing to crowds of two hundred to five hundred attendees in relatively small conference rooms. However, Dan's keynote address was to be delivered during a plenary session for all attendees in the convention center's main auditorium, capable of seating up to four thousand people.

The opening plenary session traditionally began with a thirty minute presidential address, followed by presentations — fifteen minutes each — of the top two abstracts based on voting by an international planning committee. For these plenary abstracts, the committee generally chose one that was clinically oriented — e.g., outcomes of a recent drug trial — and one that focused on basic laboratory research. Dan really could not concentrate on any of these preliminary talks as he mentally rehearsed his own presentation repeatedly. Over the years, he had probably given a thousand talks to audiences ranging in size from five to five thousand people. Irrespective of the size of the audience, he always had at least mild stage jitters. A good medical presentation was as much theater as it was science. Much like the acts of a stand-up comedian, sometimes Dan's talks were great *(I nailed that one)* and sometimes they were bad *(I really bombed)*. By the middle of a talk, he could usually assess his audience's response to tell one from the other. *I really need to nail this keynote address. Stallings might be in the audience.*

The keynote address generally started at around 10 a.m. Dan was introduced by the current president of the ISHT, Gerhard Oberauer from Germany. The co-chair of the session was the president-elect. Dan received a standing ovation both before and after his thirty-minute presentation, which focused on results of his long-term studies comparing urine assays for immunoreactive molecules in heart transplant recipients taking either cyclosporine or tacrolimus. Although this presentation represented the pinnacle of Dan's career, he found himself struggling to stifle yawns and hoped that the large crowd more appreciated the scientific basis of his talk than his jet-lagged style of presentation. He accepted the roaring applause as a positive sign and tried to think positively. He thought of Kathy. *Is your cup half-full or half empty? I thought I bombed, but the audience loved it!*

In the program break following his presentation, Dan entertained questions from dozens of curious conference attendees in the lobby outside the auditorium. He immediately broke off the question-and-answer session when he spotted Tom Stallings, literally waiting his turn in line.

"Sorry folks, I need to move on to another meeting."

In the opinions of many transplant physicians and surgeons, Tom Stallings was one of the fathers, if not *the* father of solid organ transplantation in the western hemisphere. Some in the field felt he would be a Nobel laureate some day. A masterful surgeon, he spent his early career in San Francisco developing surgical techniques for kidney and liver transplantation that remained the standards in the modern era. More importantly, he was responsible for landmark discoveries regarding mechanisms of graft rejection and of the early drugs used to prevent rejection of transplanted organs. He moved to Pittsburgh in the mid-1980s — shortly after the discovery of cyclosporine. Within ten years, he established the Pittsburgh State Transplant Institute and remained its leader until now. Although he had stopped operating several years ago, his research program remained active and he published more than ten original articles each year, not to mention innumerable textbooks and book chapters. Dan guessed that he must be approaching eighty years of age.

The fact that Dan was one of three candidates being considered to replace "the father" was exciting and humbling. The challenge of the Pittsburgh job, if Dan landed it, is that he would be responsible not just for the heart transplant program, but for all of the solid organ transplant programs: heart, lung, kidney, liver, pancreas, and small bowel. The Pittsburgh State Institute probably had the world's largest experience with multi-organ transplants, for example, liver-kidney, heart-kidney, heart-lung-kidney, liver-small bowel, and even kidney-liver-pancreas-small bowel, the latter basically consisting of removal and replacement of all essential contents within the abdominal cavity.

"I was hoping to have a moment to chat, but it seems you have another meeting to attend?" asked Dr Stallings.

"No, no. I just spotted you in line and wanted to end the question-and-answer session so we could talk. It's a real pleasure to meet you." In his three interviews in Pittsburgh, he had met virtually all of the important personnel at the Pittsburgh State Institute except for the notable Tom Stallings.

"Shall we have a cappuccino or a cup of coffee? There's a café right outside the convention center lobby."

"Of course, I have time now," said Dan.

In reality, Dan had all day. Because he was under pressure to return home for a number of reasons, he had planned this as a quick in-and-out European meeting. His only plans for the afternoon were to return to his hotel — a Sofitel just off the Champs-Elysees — catch a few hours of sleep, and then perhaps find a casual restaurant near the hotel for some red wine, cheese, and maybe some Parisian-style crème brulee — thin and crispy. Then he'd be up bright and early for his flight back home. If all went well, he would return home with more international fame and an opportunity for moving up to a world-class leadership position.

His planned itinerary needed to be pushed back to accommodate Tom Stallings. He knew that he might have an opportunity to meet him at this meeting. Hopefully, the keynote address would trigger an initial job offer — nothing official of course. *Thanks, Dr. Stallings. I'm honored by the offer. Of course, I'll need to think this over and discuss it with my family.*

Stallings started the discussion over coffee. "I very much enjoyed your address. I have been following your research from arm's length for several years now. We are particularly impressed with some of the urine assays that you've developed in Cleveland. It seems to me that some of the assays are ready for prime time — you know, large scale multicenter studies."

"Thanks. I *have* talked preliminarily to the NIH and they are interested in funding a multicenter study in this area. But they are keenly interested in broad application to *all* solid organs. Our studies, of course, have focused on heart transplant recipients but the same immune markers are probably valuable surrogate markers in kidney and liver transplant recipients, too." He was trying to create a segue to the more important topic — a job offer. The CMC excelled in heart transplants but had relatively small programs in kidney, liver, lung or pancreas transplantation. Stallings built the Pittsburgh program as a true multi-organ program, including the largest liver transplant program in the country.

"Well the PSTI would be happy to collaborate, and yes, I would think your assays could be applied to more than just heart transplantation." *Collaborate? Presumably it would be more than collaboration. I would be directing the research program.*

Dan decided to break the ice. "So I'm sure you know that I'm scheduled for another interview at the Institute in a few weeks. I'm bringing my wife. She is really looking forward to the visit." *Liar!*

"Yes — well, I'm here sort of as an emissary for the institute's search committee. Dan, your credentials are very impressive, but the institution has decided on pursuing a different route in picking the next leader of the institute."

Dan's heart began to race and he was sure that his face was flushing. "They are going with Jack Hurtuk?"

"No — and let me tell you that the discussions were long and difficult. They have chosen Henri Glotz — I am sure you know him — from right here in Paris. His wife is an American — from Chicago I think — and Henri is ready to make a move to the United States. His background is actually in bone marrow transplantation, but he has been doing pioneering work combining bone marrow transplantation with solid organ transplantation in an effort to achieve immune tolerance. He also has one of the world's most productive non-human primate laboratories — and that will fit in nicely with the current research program in Pittsburgh. I am scheduled to meet with him later this afternoon to discuss our offer. In the meantime, I am certainly hopeful that we can continue our discussions about research collaborations."

"Of course. I would love to collaborate. Hopefully, I can meet Dr. Glotz someday. *And thanks for all that background information about him — as if I wasn't aware of Glotz and his work. You really must take me for a moron.* Dr. Stallings, it was an honor to meet you. The cappuccinos are on me." *I wonder how many free cappuccinos he's had over the years.*

Although he had exchanged some U.S. dollars for francs at the airport and, as always, kept the cash in one of his front pockets, he decided to save the cash — he might need it for some serious consumption of alcohol later — and put this small bill on a credit card. When he reached to the back pocket of his suit trousers, he realized that he did not have his wallet. He was sure he had it when he left his hotel room earlier that morning. *Someone pick pocketed my wallet on the goddamn Metro!* He wanted no further embarrassment in front of Stallings and paid the bill with cash without mentioning his empty pocket.

Dan completely lost interest in the remainder of the symposium. He decided to blow it off completely and walked back, slowly and dejectedly, to his hotel. *Last time I'll ever take a subway in this city.* Negative news was building up at a rapid pace. Paris was not as beautiful as it had been in all of his previous visits. A disheveled beggar walked up to him on the Champs-Elysees asking for a few francs and Dan told him to "fuck off." He was surprised when the old man straightened up from his hunched posture and responded in perfect English, "Go fuck yourself!" *If I were only so lucky, a-hole.*

Kathy will be delighted to know that we will, with virtual certainty, spend the rest of our lives in Cleveland. He thought of calling her but remembered that it was still early in the morning back home. *I really don't want to discuss my woes with Kathy while she is half asleep. I'll wait a few hours to call.* What was supposed to be the pinnacle of his career was suddenly looking like a downward spiral. His RO1 wasn't going to be re-funded. Rick Weichel would be meeting with him soon to recommend less international travel and more time on the clinical service. When he returned, Hurtuk would be in a particularly bad mood as he would undoubtedly have learned about the Pittsburgh decision. Neither of them had suspected that Henri Glotz was on the short list. *He's not even in the mainstream of solid organ transplantation.* Oh yeah, and the Bennings case was right around the corner. Within the next month, Dan would likely go to court to defend himself against a charge of medical malpractice that could end life as he knew it. What would he do if he lost the case and the award exceeded his cap?

I'll tell you what I would do. I'd turn right around and sue Children's-CMC for Michael's Aspergillus infection and the weeks of misery it caused. I'll sue them for negligence — radiating his lungs inappropriately and threatening to take off his leg unnecessarily. I'll sue them for overdosing my son with T-cells and destroying his skin and hair. I'll sue them all! I'll get all my money back and more! That's what I'll do.

Dan heard a clap of thunder and it started to rain. *Perfect.* His anger was building. He was just denied the job opportunity of a lifetime. For his entire professional life, Dan felt like he was climbing the ladder, racing to the next level of success — higher salaries, more prestigious titles, national and international recognition. With this rejection from Pittsburgh, he would have to reassess his next career steps. Kathy had clearly become homebound. His research program just took a step backward. Patient care was less appealing these days because of all the regulations, paperwork, and threats of lawsuits. Jack Hurtuk's career was based on devotion to his patients. Dan realized now that he had slowly abandoned his patients because of his burning desire for academic success.

He had about fifty francs in his pocket — barely enough for some cheese and wine, and now he'd have to spend the rest of this lovely day in Paris making calls to cancel credit cards and to reinstate new ones so he could make his way back home. *Maybe they will not reinstall my credit cards. I could wash dishes in the kitchen and stay at this godforsaken hotel forever.*

On top of all this, Dan thought of his son, Michael; he was constantly concerned about whether Michael's latest remission would be short-lived. In July 1998, two days after the family returned from their San Francisco vacation, Michael was admitted to CMC for the third time with severe GVHD. The dermatologic manifestations — peeling of the skin, blotchy loss of hair on the head, and a vitiligo-like de-pigmentation of his torso and extremities — were more a cosmetic nuisance than a serious threat to life. But Michael went on to develop severe liver failure, one of the most dreaded complications of GVHD in which the donor T-cells attack the recipient's liver tissue. Three weeks after admission, he developed hepatic encephalopathy, a state of delirium resulting from liver failure. Michael was now into rap music, but even his favorite *Eminem* tunes at night did not help to clear the profound state of confusion caused by failure of his sick liver to clear toxins that affected the brain. The main treatment for hepatic encephalopathy was a liquid medication called lactulose — a cathartic drug that caused severe diarrhea. In healthy individuals, intestinal toxins are absorbed into the circulation, but immediately extracted by the healthy liver and metabolized into harmless molecules that were then excreted into the bile and back into the intestinal tract for elimination. The lactulose-induced diarrhea literally washed away the intestinal toxins before they could be absorbed from the intestine at all. The end result of hepatic encephalopathy and treatment with lactulose was a confused and disoriented teenage boy often sitting in a pool of liquid stool. *Lovely.*

Susan Sampson had been gradually increasing the dose of cyclosporine hoping to reverse the GVHD, but she was losing ground. Michael's liver function tests were getting worse, not better. Moreover, blood tests were showing early signs of impaired kidney function — the major side effect of cyclosporine.

In a rare effort to intervene, Dan talked to Sampson one day and asked if she had any experience using tacrolimus for GVHD. "It's a calcineurin inhibitor in the same class as cyclosporine — was just approved a few years ago, mostly for liver transplantation. We've pioneered its use in heart transplantation and also converted a few heart recipients to tacrolimus after they experienced severe rejection episodes on cyclosporine and we've been impressed. It may be more potent and possibly less nephrotoxic. Maybe it would be better than cyclosporine for GVHD."

"We've heard of it but have had no first-hand experience. At this point, I'm willing to give it a try as Michael is deteriorating and I'm not sure he can survive another episode of multi-organ failure."

Within five days of switching from cyclosporine to tacrolimus, Michael's liver function began to normalize and his acute skin lesions began to heal. His encephalopathy gradually resolved and his interest in rap music *(unfortunately)* returned.

Dan never let on to Kathy that he suggested the switch from cyclosporine to tacrolimus. He told her that cyclosporine was known to cause thickening of the gums and excessive hair growth and that Sampson suggested changing to tacrolimus to prevent those side effects.

"It's another miracle, Dan. God has blessed us with another miracle," said Kathy.

But Dan no longer believed in miracles. Sure, it was medically incredible that Michael survived two bouts of AML and a severe episode of GHVD resulting from an overdose of his sister's T-cells. But he chalked it up to medical technology, the wonders of the human body, and incredibly good luck.

Michael was currently doing well, albeit prone to frequent colds and episodes of bronchitis and ear infections. His GVHD left him with some patchy alopecia — so in his early twenties Michael elected to go with the Jordan look, shaving his head bald on a regular basis to hide the patchy bald spots. His vitiligo had receded to involve only some small areas of de-pigmentation around the many surgical scars on his torso — most of which were hidden by standard clothing. There had been some concern that the chest surgeries and radiation might decrease his pulmonary capacity. But save for a ticklish cough and the tendency to get bronchitis, he did not seem overly compromised. Yes, Michael was alive and reasonably healthy, but Dan lived in constant fear of the next fever, the next phone call, the next surprise. Okay, maybe it was a miracle — but how many miracles does one family get?

It was only early afternoon in Paris, but Dan got back to his hotel room, removed his soaking wet suit coat, and convinced himself that he needed a drink. *What the hell, it's five o'clock somewhere.* He unloaded the memory sticks and laser pointer from his pockets, loosened his tie, and opened the minibar. No Glenlivet, but those bottles of Johnny Walker were looking mighty good — even if only Johnny Walker *Red.* He poked his head into the hallway. *Of course, no ice machines. This is fricking Europe.* He decided to undress completely and prepared his bed for a long nap after a little drink. He poured himself two miniature bottles of Johnny Walker — served neat, thank you — and turned on his television, quickly finding the CNN channel.

Two jet planes had just flown into the World Trade Center towers in New York City.

Twenty-One

Solon Ohio —
September 11, 2001

Kathy liked to exercise at the Solon Oaks Fitness Club early in the morning. During the school year, that meant right after the kids left for school. She would be done with her exercise by 10:00 a.m. and ready for whatever the day had in store — cleaning, washing clothes, shopping, and preparing meals. Michael was now eighteen years old but after missing almost two years of school, had been held back so that he was now only a junior at Solon High School, just one year ahead of the twins. All three of the younger children now had their drivers' licenses and Kathy and Dan were happy to let them drive to school together in the old family Taurus. Kathy was particularly delighted to be relieved of the chauffer's job that she had for many years. Tom was still home for the summer and planned to spend the day packing as his mother volunteered to drive him back to Ohio State the next day to begin his junior year.

Toward the end of her seven-mile power walk on the tread-mill, Kathy was in the middle of her usual jovial chat with her elderly man-friends Tom and John — sharing recipes and chat-ting about family matters and recent trips. Tom was a retired bank president and John a retired accountant. Both were rela-tively affluent, traveled often, and loved hearing about Kathy's trips with her husband. The club was crowded and the sounds emanating from the overhead television monitors were relatively subdued by the morning chatter. When Kathy glanced up to see a jet plane crashing into one of the World Trade Center towers, she presumed it was a sci-fi movie of some kind. Then a second plane crashed into the second tower. *Incredible special effects.* A few minutes later, every television monitor in the club seemed to be running delayed versions of the scene. *I can't believe ev-eryone wants to watch the same silly sci-fi movie.* She quickly ended her workout when she realized, along with the other club members, that they were witnessing more than a science fiction movie. They all huddled around the large flat-screen TV in the club's lounge and watched the events of the morning unfold. There were some obscene comments about terrorists but most club members were silent and several women openly sobbed.

Kathy immediately thought of Dan, quickly showered, and left the club.

Driving home, she mentally calculated the time difference between Ohio and France *(Damn, did Dan say it was five hours or six?)* and roughly figured that Dan must have landed in Paris safely long before the catastrophe in New York. *But what if there was a flight delay? That happens all the time in Newark — and Newark is a mere stone's throw away from the site of the ter-rorist attack. President Bush had quickly cancelled all flights in and out of U.S. airports. What if Dan was still in the air when the attacks began? Would they force his plane to return to the United States? Or maybe land prematurely in Spain or the United Kingdom? What if the terrorists were attacking the entire world? Certainly Paris would be a prime target in Europe.*

She called Continental Airlines to inquire about the status of Dan's flight but only got a recording. *"Your call is important to us but all of our agents are busy now; please stay on the line."* Obviously, millions of people were just as concerned as Kathy about their traveling loved ones and the phone lines were jammed. As she was redialing, the kids walked in — school was cancelled for the remainder of the day.

Michael turned on the television in the family room. The scene in downtown New York was chaotic. The news coverage suddenly shifted to a different location. Another jet had crashed into the Pentagon. Kathy's anxiety accelerated a couple of notches.

Tom had been sleeping in but was awakened by all the chatter. He strolled into the family room wearing his night clothes (same as his day clothes) and was quickly updated by his family.

"Jesus, it looks like the whole country is under attack," said Tom.

Lauren stood up and said, "Maybe it's not just an attack on our country; maybe it's a world attack — the beginning of World War Three." She went to her mother and hugged her. "Mom, have you heard from Dad?"

Ironically, Dan had recently talked about getting international cell phone service or even a satellite phone but decided that the expense was unwarranted, even with his current level of travel activity. He almost always arranged to call home at least every other day when he was traveling. But because he was planning on being in Paris for less than twenty-four hours, he told Kathy that he would skip an overseas phone call from France and call her only when he got back into Newark on September 12, after she returned from the morning trip to Columbus. How much can happen in twenty-four hours that would warrant an overseas call? *Really, how much can happen in a day?*

Kathy hugged Lauren back and replied, "No. God knows if he's even aware of what's going on. He's probably in the middle of his conference. Maybe he's giving his talk right now. Or maybe they cancelled the conference. Or maybe they really don't care what happens to Americans over in Paris. You know what? I don't even know which hotel Dad is staying at in Paris. It was supposed to be a one-day trip. I'm sure he'll call us as soon as he knows what's going on over here."

After being on hold for twenty-five minutes, a human voice from Continental Airlines finally got on the line with Kathy: Yes, Dan's flight had arrived safely in Paris — No there have been no reports of terrorist attacks in Europe — All Continental flights from Europe to the United States were cancelled for *at least* the next twenty-four hours and possibly longer — With the expected back up, it could take several days for U.S. travelers in Europe to get back home — Yes, let's hope we've seen the end of the attacks.

One of the towers collapsed and New York City was in state of pandemonium. The destruction was beyond the imagination of most Americans. It was too early to even think about how many people died or were dying. Eight million people in New York were probably worrying to death about what building would be hit next by a jet airplane. Watching all of this on a TV screen was surrealistic.

Tom chimed in, "Mom, change the channel. I just heard on the radio that there's been another plane crash in Pennsylvania."

World War Three was now close to home.

Twenty-Two

Paris —
September 11, 2001

Dan never took his nap as he was mesmerized, like the rest of the world, by the events happening in the United States. He also suddenly found himself between an inconceivable rock and a hard place. He still had his passport, having left it in his hotel safe earlier in the morning. But his hope that just maybe he left his wallet in his room was quickly dashed. Indeed, his wallet must have been stolen — probably on the crowded subway. He had lost credit cards before and the process of reinstating them was usually straightforward: Call the company, cancel the stolen card number immediately so that the thief would not have time to purchase a yacht or a Hummer before you discovered the loss.

The problem was that seemingly the entire business world had come to a complete halt because of the terrorist attacks in the United States. He could not get through to either VISA, Master-Card, or Diners Club. From television coverage, he understood that his flight to Newark — and for that matter *all* flights to the United States scheduled for the next twenty-four hours — would be cancelled. Frustrated with phone calls that yielded only apologetic recordings, he decided to talk instead to the front desk at the hotel about extending his stay.

"Yes, Monsieur, we have a sudden crisis with many travelers like you who are stranded. Unfortunately, we are fully occupied for tomorrow night. However, we can accommodate you in one of our sister Sofitel hotels near Montmartre. I will just need some identification and a credit card."

Jesus.

He explained the dilemma he had and promised to return after he made contact with one of his credit card companies. He thought of calling Continental Airlines to book a new flight but it was unlikely that they would be booking any new flights soon until the presidential ban was lifted. Besides, to book a new flight he would need — a credit card.

He returned to his room — at least it was booked for tonight. He opened the minibar. He had polished off three scotches but there was still one miniature Jack Daniels, two vodkas and one gin. He popped open one of the vodkas and sipped it slowly. He pulled out his traveling CD player and headphones and popped in a CD he had burned with a medley of Dick's Picks: live versions of the Grateful Dead's "China Cat Sunflower," "I Know You Rider," "Scarlet Begonias," and "Fire on the Mountain." After the second miniature bottle of Smirnoff's and the single miniature bottle of Beefeaters' gin, he fell asleep — tired and drunk.

* * *

Dan rarely conversed with strangers on planes. Generally, when he recognized that he had a "talker" sitting next to him, he'd pull out his laptop or a folder of papers to provide strong signals that he needed to work and that he had no interest in chatting. He was returning home on an overnight "red eye" flight from Los Angeles to Cleveland after giving a talk at UCLA — first-class window seat — 1A bulkhead. He pulled out three papers from recent journals. He had intended to have a scotch or two, read the manuscripts and then attempt to get a couple hours of sleep. It looked like the aisle seat — 1B — was going to be empty, but just before the cabin door was closed a young man walked on the plane and took the seat. He appeared to be in his late twenties, thin, with shoulder length dark hair — looked just like Jim Morrison in his early years with the Doors. He was wearing a tie-dyed T-shirt, stylish blue jeans, a slick black leather coat, and expensive-looking brown leather shoes — *maybe Florentine?* Unlike virtually every other passenger, he walked on the plane completely empty handed — no carry-ons, no laptop, no electronic devices of any kind.

Dan had already been sipping on his first scotch–on-the-rocks. The newcomer ordered tomato juice before the flight took off, leaned over Dan's papers and said, "You must be a doctor."

Here we go. Nothing worse than a talker on a red eye.

"Yes I am." He couldn't resist, recalling that they were in L.A. after all: "And you must be a rock star?"

"No. I wish. I am retired. I'm actually heading to my apartment in New York, but need to stop in Cleveland to buy a car. An old man living in Beachwood owned a custom-built Bentley and kept it in his garage untouched for almost twenty years. He passed away a couple of months ago and the family has the car up for auction. I've never been to Cleveland, let alone Beachwood. Are you heading home? Do you know where Beachwood is?"

Dan's interest was piqued — it was late, but he couldn't have misjudged the man's age that badly. *Retired?* If this young chap was going to chat, he was anticipating a "dude bomb." In fact, he spoke softly and intelligently.

"Sure. East side suburb — maybe ten miles from the city — twenty miles from the airport. Did you say you're retired?"

"Yes. I just walked away from it all a year ago. And I've never been happier."

"Walked away from what?"

"Do you go to movies in theaters?"

"Rarely, maybe once a year." Dan honestly couldn't remember the last time he was in a movie theater. He remembered seeing James Bond in *Live and Let Die* on maybe his third date with Kathy many years ago. These days, they mostly watched movies on cable TV or very rarely rented or bought a movie on VHS to be played at home. Somehow going to movies in theaters had become a thing of their distant past.

"Well, have you seen the cardboard stand-ups in the lobbies of theaters? They are like stand-up posters that advertise coming attractions — mostly picturing the actors and actresses in some action scene from an upcoming feature film — paintings, not photographs."

Dan lied, "Yeah, sure."

"I chose art school over college when I finished high school and started painting lobby stand-ups as a hobby. My mother worked for one of the big studios in L.A., loved my stand-ups, and showed them to a few friends. Before I turned twenty, I had a profitable one-man business, producing stand-ups for thirty or forty theaters in southern California. I then expanded the business by hiring some young commercial artists and going regional, then national. My mother quit her job at the studio and managed the company. I won't say that the company has a monopoly, but we certainly are the dominant stand-up producer in the United States. When I walked away, we had offices in L.A., Chicago, and New York — over one hundred employees — profits were over ten million a year."

Dan could not believe how engaged he was by this young man. While telling the story of his career, the plane had taken off and the flight attendant was already offering the second round of drinks — another scotch and a second tomato juice.

"So why did you walk away?"

"Life is short. I'm almost thirty and have a beautiful wife and two small kids. We have homes in Malibu and Maui, and a three-bedroom apartment on the Upper West Side of Manhattan. In nine years, I made more money than I'll ever need. Now I paint for fun and I collect old cars — some of which I fix and sell — so I still have some income. Oh yeah, and in the last two years, I've started writing.

"What kind of writing?"

"Short stories, a couple of novels in progress. I write when I'm in the mood — there is no hurry, no deadline. It clears my mind — hard to explain. I write mostly for myself and let my wife read the fictional stuff. Someday, I may try to publish it."

Three scotch-on-the-rocks later, Dan realized that he had been transfixed by this young man's conversation. His life seemed to be perfect — almost too perfect — and he was one of happiest human beings he had ever met — and not yet even thirty years old.

When the pilot announced their initial descent into the Cleveland area, Dan couldn't believe how fast the four-and-a-half-hour flight went by. It was 6:30 a.m. Cleveland time and the sky was beginning to brighten to the east. As was often the case, northeast Ohio was covered in clouds and the pilot announced a temperature of 43 degrees, rain, and low visibility at Cleveland Hopkins Airport. The plane vectored out over Lake Erie about ten miles east of the city for a northeast-to-southwest landing. It seemed to take longer than usual for the plane to break through the lower ceiling of clouds and, to say the least, the descent was very turbulent. Finally, Dan could make out city structures below and was horrified — the jet plane was no more than a few hundred feet above the ground and was aiming directly for the mid-section of the Terminal Tower.

* * *

He awakened and sat bolt upright in a cold sweat, still drunk from a bad mixture of scotch, vodka, and gin. He grabbed his throbbing head. *Oh my God — just a dream.* He fell back to a supine position, trying to decide whether the dream was very bad or very good.

Twenty-Three

Solon, Ohio — September 14, 2001

Over the course of three days, Kathy's frame of mind gradually changed from being a little worried to being mildly panic stricken. She was thinking that maybe Dan had called while she was driving to and back from Columbus two days ago. But when she got home there were no messages. She checked her cell phone every few hours to make sure the batteries were still charged. He was not calling and she had no way of calling him. During business hours, she called Dan's secretary every couple of hours hoping for some word.

"Mrs. Ulek, we are all concerned here, too, but rest assured that I will call you immediately if we hear from your husband," Norma promised. Amazingly, Dan also had not told Norma where he was staying in Paris — presumably because the trip was so short. Dan made the one-day hotel arrangements through some European travel agent and Norma had no number or any clue about their location.

Kathy called Jack Hurtuk at home that night, hoping for some clues.

"No, Kathy, I haven't had any communication with Dan either. No, he didn't tell me where he would be staying. Through the grapevine, I've heard about several national colleagues who were at the same meeting in Paris. Most of them will be stranded for three to five days because of the backlog of travelers needing to fly home. So I'm not sure why Dan hasn't called, but chances are he'll be flying back in the next day or so. By the way, word has it that he gave a great talk at the meeting. *I hope that will cheer her up.* Apparently, the meeting organizers decided to cancel the rest of the symposium later that afternoon because of world events. What an awful catastrophe."

"Yes, awful," said Kathy, beginning to wonder if Dan might have gone off the deep end after pondering the state of the world following the plane crashes in New York, D.C., and Pennsylvania.

She called Dan's mother.

"Sorry to be calling so late, but I still haven't heard from Dan and I'm worried sick. All summer long, I worried that Dan looked depressed, and — well — I'm just worried sick that something bad is happening. Certainly phone lines around the world are working now. I just can't imagine why he hasn't tried calling."

"Can I interest you in a cup of tea?"

It was late, but Kathy really appreciated the opportunity to vent with another adult. Rose Ulek lived only five minutes away. That's one of the reasons why Dan wanted to move to Solon. "Sure, Ma, that would be great. I'll be there in ten minutes."

Rose spoke first over tea. "This little circumstance reminds me of some of Ed's little escapades."

Kathy was aware that her father-in-law had psychiatric problems, but aside from his intermittently depressed appearance and Dan's discussion about his medications, she really never discussed details with either Dan or his mother.

"Ed was bipolar. He mostly had long periods of depression but every year or two he would go through episodes of mania. He was actually quite pleasant during the early phases of those manic episodes — energetic, amusing, even playful. But eventually he would get out of control. On several occasions, he just dropped out of sight — sometimes for just hours or less than a day — but a couple of times for up to two weeks. Kathy, I'm not even sure if Dan was aware of these disappearing acts. The first few times, I panicked — called the cops, the whole nine yards. But Ed always came back. Usually he apologized quickly and insincerely, and life went on. And let's just say that he made it very clear that his whereabouts were not open for discussion. To this day, I have no idea where he went or what he did on these little adventures. I always did the monthly bills — even when Ed was still alive — and scoured them for clues — you know, motel bills, entertainment bills, bills from liquor stores — but I never found anything suspicious. So he must have had his own stash of cash, or maybe some generous friends. After several years, when he disappeared, I got to the point of caring less — in fact I kind of enjoyed my little vacations with Ed away."

Kathy realized that she had never had a really serious conversation with her mother-in-law before. She was intrigued but also scared.

"Anyhow, all of these episodes were precipitated by some kind of stress — you know, money issues, bills, marital issues — well, what the hell, just between you and me Kath, Ed had erection problems for twenty years, so I'm pretty sure he was not having affairs — at least not with women. The point is, this bipolar stuff tends to run in families. I know Dan was working long hours all summer, but — I hope I'm not being too nosey — has he been under any unusual stresses recently?"

Wow — loaded question. I'm not sure how much she needs to know. Erections? No problem there. Job stress? Always. Pressure from his division chief? Big time. Add a pending lawsuit, wham. And then of course there was the Pittsburgh — Oh my God, that's it!

"Oh yeah, that's it, Ma — can't believe how stupid I've been. Dan has been interviewing for a big position at the University of Pittsburgh — the Transplant Institute there. He told me he might meet the current program director at the meeting in Paris — Dr. Starling, Stinchcomb — whatever. I'm sure that's it — he probably met with this doctor . . ." *But what announcement would send him over the deep end? Rejection — maybe. But if they offered him the position —*

"Oh gees, Ma, the night before he left, I told Dan that I didn't want to move to Pittsburgh. He may be sitting in Paris wondering whether he should leave me to take the job of a lifetime. Damnit, this is all my fault. And I don't even know where he is staying or how to call him."

She called Jack Hurtuk's office the next morning and caught him between cases in the operating room.

"Hi, Kathy. Any word from Dan?"

"No. Jack, can I ask a somewhat personal question?"

"Sure. Go ahead."

"Have there been any decisions about that director's job in Pittsburgh in the past week or so?"

"Well, I didn't want to bring this up when we talked yesterday, but yes, I got a call from the University provost two days ago telling me that I was no longer on their short list. Kathy, I didn't bring it up, but as a proud and aging surgeon I guess I hated to admit it — seems likely to me that they offered the job to Dan. But then, I presumed he would have been more anxious than ever to call you and let you know."

So that was it — Dan was just offered the Pittsburgh position and sat depressed in a Paris hotel knowing that his wife did not want to make a move. Kathy was completely frustrated, having no way to contact her husband — until . . .

She had an idea. Despite the fact that her husband and children were all proficient with the use of computers and other electronic devices, Kathy remained computer-ignorant, barely knowing how to turn on a PC. Two years ago, she was embarrassed when her Solon Oaks man-friends offered to send her recipes via e-mail. She reluctantly asked Dan to teach her how to use e-mail. Dan set up a Yahoo e-mail account. "Write this down somewhere: your username is easy — kathy.ulek. That makes your e-mail address kathy.ulek@yahoo.com. Now you'll need a password. Let's think of one that you'll never forget — got it — ilovedan. Okay, got it? Username — kathy.ulek, password — ilovedan."

Kathy was totally confused. Since when did *periods* become *dots*? Why are there dots in some names but not others? Why didn't she capitalize the letters in her codename or password or whatever it was called? For one week, she sat with Dan each night exchanging recipes with her man-friends. Thereafter, she would tell Dan how much fun she was having using e-mail on a daily basis to keep in touch with friends — but in reality, she decided that computers and e-mail were not for her and she gave it up.

"Brian, can you help me check my e-mail?"

"Sure, Mom. Do you use Yahoo or AOL?"

"Yahoo of course *(I think)*, but I've forgotten my codenames."

"Codename — you mean your password?"

"Yes, I meant password. I somehow forgot my password for crying out loud."

Brian figured out her username quickly enough as it was pretty standard. Staring at the computer screen and the Yahoo home page, Kathy now had a vivid memory of her sessions with Dan and her password — ilovedan.

Sitting in front of the computer screen, Kathy looked at her youngest son and noticed that his color was off.

"Hey, kiddo, are you feeling all right?" she asked.

"I'm okay, Mom — a little stomach ache the past few days. And feeling a little tired."

Of all the kids, Brian seemed the most blown away by the terrorist attacks three days earlier, and Kathy knew that, for Brian, anxiety often translated into physical ailments.

"You wanna lie down and take a nap before dinner?"

"Yeah, good idea. Honestly, I'm not very hungry though. Are you okay with your e-mail now?"

"Thanks, Brian, I can take it from here," said Kathy, now a little worried about her youngest son.

Sure enough, she typed in her password and more than twenty e-mails appeared, some more than a year old. The first dozen or so were from Tom and John — mostly recipes and family news. Some referred to "attached" photographs, but she had no idea what that meant or how to view the photos. She then saw the most recent e-mail from daniel.ulek, dated September 13, and opened it.

The message was short and emotionless:

"Hello, Kathy. I am heading for Chateau Eza in the morning. Please meet me there as soon as possible. I have an important decision to discuss with you. I have transferred money into the National City account to cover the expense. I may not have access to e-mail."

Chateau Eza! Either he wants to romance me into moving to Pittsburgh or indeed he has gone off the deep end. One way or another, this was very abnormal behavior for her husband. Maybe Dan was having a manic episode like his father's. She needed to work this out with him. Obviously, he had already decided that he had no intention of working it out by way of a phone call. *Oh, Dan, if this job is so important to you, yes, I would be willing to move to Pittsburgh. Why can't you just call me and I'll tell you.* She knew she was going to have to travel to France. Her husband, her marriage and her life hung in the balance.

Twenty-Four

Eze, France —
September 16-17, 2001

Kathy called Rose Ulek and asked her to watch the kids. "I got a cryptic e-mail from Dan. I think your theory may be correct. He left Paris and is staying in a hotel on the French Riviera. We visited the same place several years ago during a vacation. I called the hotel and they say he is registered but he is not answering the phone. I'm really worried about his mental health. I'm going to meet him there and work this out."

"Oh, and Ma, I kept Brian home from school today — he's had a stomach flu for the past few days. Please keep an eye on him. I'm leaving the hotel phone number on the refrigerator door — call me any time if you need to. I'll try calling you as soon as I get checked in."

Earlier, Kathy had called her sister-in-law, Rita, who worked for a travel agency. Throughout her married life, Dan had always made all of their travel arrangements. On the few occasions when she traveled alone, Dan still made the arrangements for airline tickets, car rentals, etc. She realized that she had no clue how to arrange air travel and was happy to have Rita in the family.

Of course, she had to stretch the truth about her sudden need for tickets to Nice, France —especially at a time like this with the world going crazy.

"Dan got stuck in France after the September 11 attacks, so he made this impulsive decision for a romantic little vacation, now that the flying ban has been lifted."

"Well, Kathy, under normal circumstances you might have had trouble getting tickets to Europe on such short notice. But right now, the airplanes are wide open because most folks are afraid to fly. I wish your brother was as romantic as Dan. Sounds like fabulous fun. Are you going to need a car rental?"

"Yes — oh cripes — can you get a car with an automatic shift?"

Instead, she hired a limo service to meet her outside of the customs area in the Nice Airport — very expensive, but Dan had transferred five thousand dollars into the checking account *(must have been a generous honorarium for the Paris talk)*. Besides, she figured that she only needed a one-way drive from Nice to Eze as she would either be staying or leaving somewhere with her crazy husband. And sitting in the back seat of the limo gave her time to collect her thoughts while once again enjoying the visual delights of the Cote d'Azur.

The driver dropped her off at the foot of the hill that rose steeply upward to the medieval village. She had only her purse and a small suitcase, having packed casual clothes for a two-day trip. She immediately recalled her previous visit to this magical and romantic place — flowers and cacti, open markets, and cobblestone streets. Dan had told her that she was "more beautiful than ever" or some such nonsense during their lunch overlooking the Mediterranean Sea. Her heart was now racing, in part from the upward walk to the Chateau, but mostly in anticipation of seeing Dan — her husband, her lover, and her best friend.

She stopped to catch her breath before entering the hotel's lobby. Fortunately, the receptionist spoke English.

"I am looking for Dan Ulek's room. I am Mrs. Ulek, his wife."

"Madam, Dr. Ulek is registered here but he left a message two days ago saying that he would be gone for the day. He also left this package. If I can see your passport, I will happily give you the keys to the room. And madam, there is a second phone message here from a Mrs. Rose Ulek."

He handed her an envelope and an 8½ x 11-inch package, about two inches thick, wrapped in brown paper.

She checked into her room, hardly noticing the delightful furnishings, spacious balcony, and the lovely view of the Mediterranean Sea. She opened the envelope and read the message:

"Dear Kathy:

We've been through a lot, and this summer has been particularly stressful. I decided to write a book about all of this. Here's a copy for you.

Love,
Dan"

The second phone message from her mother-in-law read:

"Please call home about Brian."

Part II

Twenty-Five

Chateau Eza —
September 17, 2001

What the hell is going on? Kathy looked around the room. It was Dan's room for sure. A pair of familiar and obviously worn briefs (read: tire tracks) and socks adorned a corner of the room. *Will he ever grow up and change his male habits?* In the bathroom, she found some, but not all of Dan's toiletries — a hair brush and bottle of cologne. The other essentials and his usual toiletry bag were missing. She carefully examined the rest of the room. Dan's briefcase and suitcase were nowhere to be found. There were two empty wine bottles in the bathroom wastebasket. On the desk she found two USB memory sticks, a laser pointer, and some loose papers — most with scribbled notes and doodles.

She decided to be patient and to do nothing for at least twenty-four hours. After all, the hotel receptionist had reported that Dan would be "gone for the day." Surely, he'll show up any minute now and explain his crazy behavior, talk to me about his troubles, let me be his wife and help him work through all of this.

With virtually nothing else to do, she started to read Dan's book. She got through three or four chapters and recognized that it was vaguely an autobiographical novel, but with many unfamiliar details. The title and the early chapters clearly revolved around a doctor's angst about a professional move to Pittsburgh, but the names and faces were all changed. *This is all my fault! The man has been tormented.*

Later that morning, she decided that it was time to notify the local authorities. It was easier said than done, in part because of the language barrier *(three years of high school French and what good does it do me now?)* and a definite hint of good old-fashioned French anti-Americanism. Bottom line: without any solid evidence of foul play, there was not much that the local police could do.

In the afternoon, she called home to check on Brian, and also called the CMC to see if they had any word from Dan. Nothing.

Rose sounded a little concerned about Brian. "I kept him home again today. He's keeping down soup and liquids but he's feverish and looks pale."

"Well, we're going into the weekend, so just be sure he stays home and rests and maybe try a couple of Tylenol." She had a sudden flashback to December 1994, recalling the initial symptom's of Michael's illness. *Don't go there. Lightning never strikes twice. I'm sure it's just the flu. Just a virus.*

"So what are you going to do about Dan, dear?" asked Rose Ulek.

"I really don't know." She had about twelve hours to make a decision. Her return flight home from Nice was scheduled for late the next morning. She would need to call the limo service soon to make plans for the trip back to Nice Airport. She could cancel the return flight and sit tight in her hotel room waiting to hear something from Dan, but she might go insane herself if all this lasted more than another day. She honestly wondered if she would ever see her husband again.

As she ended the call with Rose, Kathy found herself sitting at the room's desk and fumbling through the loose papers that Dan had left there. At the very bottom of the pile, there was a printed copy of an e-mail from Dr. Tom Kingsfield, dated September 9, 2001:

> "Dan:
> I didn't realize you were going out of town. Please call me as soon as you can. I received the results of your routine CBC: Hematocrit 24 percent, Platelets 15,000, WBC 23,400 with 5 percent blasts. You need to see a hematologist as soon as you get back.
>
> Tom Kingsfield"

Oh sweet Jesus. Can this really be happening? Kathy had become an expert at interpreting complete blood counts and immediately recognized the diagnosis — leukemia. *Did it run in families? Was this a complete coincidence? What the hell motivated him to return to Eze? Did he get this e-mail before or after coming here? And where the hell is he? And why the hell is he not trying to communicate with me?*

Is the man that I have known and loved capable of committing suicide?

It was approaching 9 p.m. in France and she suddenly realized that she had not slept for almost twenty-four hours. Still waiting for the phone to ring, she took a hot shower, changed into her nightgown, and crawled into bed pondering the day's events. She slept poorly because of jet lag and despite trying one of Dan's old tricks: Benadryl and brandy. She sat up fitfully and stared out into the sea below.

She picked up Dan's manuscript and continued reading. There was really *nothing* else to do. She was touched by his accounts of Michael's illness — revealing some of the feelings that he never shared at the time. She stopped when she read the passage: *If I ever developed this disease, I would refuse all treatment, take care of my affairs, buy a case of Glenlivet, and try to enjoy the remaining few months of my life.* There was no Scotch in the room, but now she was truly alarmed.

The phone rang at 4:30 a.m. — it was the receptionist at the front desk.

"So sorry for bothering you at this hour, Madam, but I have an urgent call from Dr. Ulek. Can you take the call?"

She had a sudden adrenaline rush followed by a fainting sensation, but replied calmly, "Yes, I can take the call."

"Kathy? I love you so much. Please don't talk until you hear me out. I'm sick. I did not intend to leave you in the dark. I can explain everything. I miss you and need to see you to explain it all."

"Dan. Not another word of explanation. You can't imagine how happy I am to hear your voice *(and to know that you are alive)*. All I want to know right now is where the hell you are."

"I'm back in Paris — at Hopital Necker. It's a long story. Please check out and come here today."

"But I have a ticket from Nice to Newark later today."

"You'll have to cancel."

The last time she heard those words from Dan, it marked the beginning of a four-year ordeal.

"Dan, I saw the e-mail from Tom Kingsfield on your hotel room desk. I'm no doctor, but I'm an expert on complete blood counts."

"We'll talk about it. I just want you here with me as soon as possible. Fastest way to get here is by train. The hotel receptionist can tell you how to do it. Are you good for money?"

"Yes."

"Take the earliest train. You can be here by evening. I'll explain everything when you get here. I love you, Kathy."

She wrote down the address and more details about getting to Hopital Necker via train and taxi. Of course, there was no use trying to sleep. The sun would be rising in another hour. She showered, dressed, and packed her bags. While waiting for the break of dawn, she continued to read Dan's novel.

Twenty-Six

New York, May 2001

Kathy and Dan hopped into a taxi at the Marquis and headed back to LaGuardia. Dan thought Kathy appeared pensive but presumed that it was just end-of-the-weekend blues until she spoke up.

"Are you happy, Dan?"

He paused before answering, trying to anticipate her concern. "Sure, it was a great weekend, didn't you think?"

"I'm not talking about the weekend. You've seemed distracted for months. And why haven't you told me about the Pittsburgh job?"

"Kath, I've had lots of job offers in the past two years — too many to bother telling you about. I haven't taken any of them seriously."

"Nancy Hurtuk tells me this job may be different. You didn't tell me that Jack Hurtuk is also being considered."

"Sorry hon, I just didn't think any of this would interest you."

"Dan, you can't divorce your professional life from your family life. You've been stressed for months now. Only today do I find out about this big lawsuit. You told me you were giving a talk at Pittsburgh and I only find out through Nancy that it's actually a job interview. Now you're going on service for three straight months and I'm worried whether you'll come out of summer as the same man I married. Is there anything else about your life that you're hiding from me?"

Dan wasn't prepared for this line of questions. And the last one had undertones of infidelity — kind of surprising after a weekend of lovemaking. He decided to ignore that vibration.

"I wasn't going to bring up the lawsuit until it turned out to be serious — as I only learned from Jack earlier today. As far as Pittsburgh goes, I can't imagine that I am a serious candidate for the position — there are probably a dozen more qualified candidates and I'm almost certain that they are looking for a surgeon to replace Tom Stallings. But you know, Kathy, sometimes I like to think big — is that so bad?"

"You don't like being in Cleveland, do you? I forced you to come back."

"It's my hometown."

"But you've never had any burning desire to return to or stay in your hometown. Family has never meant the same thing to you as it does to me. I feel like I'm holding you back from busting that move that you talked about years ago."

"Not at all," he lied. "We've built a great transplant program at CMC and I've become internationally known for my research based on my work with Jack. It probably wouldn't have materialized in a different environment. Besides, living in Cleveland provides a good reason for traveling and vacationing more often to get away."

That attempt at a joke did nothing to change Kathy's concerns. Her husband seemed stressed and increasingly depressed.

But she remained devoted to him and hoped that she could retain his own devotion.

"That's not funny, Dan. I hope you know I love you to pieces. But please don't feel that you need to keep secrets from me, okay."

"Promise," he replied, thinking about the novels that he was writing secretly. *Maybe I should hold off on getting them published.*

Twenty-seven

St. Tropez, France — July 2003

Kathy moved toward the sunroom carrying a serving platter with a plate full of strawberry crepes and fresh brewed coffee for Lauren and Brian. It was so nice having them stay for the summer. Both of them would be heading for college back home in the fall. She was hoping that Tom also could have joined them for the summer, but he was now working back in Ohio. Maybe next year. The term "sunroom" was a misnomer — the room was twice the size of their family room in Solon and the vistas were spectacular. There were five acres of property covered with olive and fig trees, with the beach and the ultra-blue Mediterranean Sea a few hundred yards further beyond. She found Lauren engaged on the Internet. Brian was curled up in the big leather sofa, reading a book.

"Perfect timing, Mom, I just finished another one of Dad's books," said Brian.

"Oh? Which one?"

"*A Trip to Pittsburgh.* Is this the one he handed to you after 9-11?"

"Yep, did you like it?"

Until her second trip to Eze, Kathy never appreciated that her husband was a closet writer. Of course, he had authored or co-authored more than two hundred peer-reviewed manuscripts in medical journals as well as hundreds of abstracts and dozens of medical books and book chapters. So she often saw Dan composing manuscripts on his computer, but she had been unaware that he had *creative* writing skills. God knows when he found the time to express them — nights, weekends, maybe during his many trips away.

By the fall of 2001, he had written three novels — each with medical themes. The first two dealt with interactions between internists, surgeons, and malpractice lawyers, and each ended with suicides or suicidal ideations. Originally, writing was no more than a hobby and a form of relieving stress for Dan. An editor of one of his cardiology textbooks learned that Dan had written a novel, asked to read the manuscript, and first suggested that he consider publication. He spent several months trying unsuccessfully to pitch his first two books to literary agents in the United States, most often receiving rubber stamp rejections. Among the few U.S. agents who offered to read his manuscripts, only one — a woman working at an obscure agency in Alaska — was polite enough to reply by e-mail several weeks later: "Your work is dry and uninteresting. I suggest that you go back to saving lives and stop wasting your time writing novels." *Talk about deflating. Why doesn't she just grab my balls and twist them off!* As a last-ditch effort, he submitted his first two books to Redicon — a publishing house in the United Kingdom — and received some favorable comments and reviews. After submitting his third novel, "A Trip to Pittsburgh," Redicon wrote to him with an offer to buy the rights for his first three books and

100,000 pounds in advance as part of a contract to produce three more novels in the next three years. He sent a copy of the offer letter to Alaska.

Brian sighed and said, "Yes, I loved it. The end was surprising but sad. I was ready to ball my eyes out before you walked in with breakfast. This is the best of Dad's stuff that I've read so far but I'm not sure why he is so infatuated with suicide. Was the story about Michael coughing up blood against the wall really true?"

"I'm afraid so," said Kathy, trying to repress the memory of that awful day.

"Is that fresh coffee I smell?" It was Dan, stepping out of his art studio and into the sun room — wearing khaki brown trousers, an old flannel shirt covered with oil paint and turpentine stains, and no socks or shoes.

Kathy took a look at Dan. *Fashion flaws aside, he looks better now than the day we got married.* Indeed, after recovering from chemotherapy and an accompanying twenty-five pound weight loss, he embarked upon a daily exercise program and managed to keep the weight down while building some muscle mass. He would do some power walking with Kathy in the mornings and often take long walks on the beach after dinner. With the weight loss, he was able to wean himself off blood pressure medicines and he felt more fit than ever — now having a handsome, gaunt appearance.

Michael walked in the side door wearing running shorts and an Ohio State T-shirt, downing a bottle of water, and covered with sweat after an early morning run on the beach. He was also staying for most of the summer, but would return in the fall for his junior year at Bowling Green State University, hoping to apply to nursing school after graduation. He looked healthy but still shaved his head daily to hide his patchy alopecia. In four months, he would be a nine-year survivor of AML.

"Well, I hope all you Uleks have been feeding your brains with books and the Internet while I was out doing five-and-a-half miles," Michael said a bit arrogantly.

"Michael, that's awesome — almost a 10K!" said Kathy. For years, she was concerned that lung surgeries and unnecessary radiation would make Michael a pulmonary cripple, but slowly and surely he proved her concerns to be unfounded, and he was almost as athletic now as he was as a ten-year-old.

"Well, you know brother dear, ND requires each of us to read at least twelve books for the summer before freshman year," Lauren said. "I've already read eleven and Brian is now up to thirteen — but I'm not sure if ND accepts books by parents."

Both of the twins got accepted to Notre Dame. *Not exactly the Ivy League, but not too shabby.* Dan was really proud of the twins and all of his children.

"Hey, Dad, I just finished *A Trip to Pittsburgh*," said Brian. "Don't you believe in happy endings?"

"Oh, that's just fiction, Michael. Someday I'll write a book that tells the real story."

Twenty-Eight

Eze and Paris —
September 12-17, 2001

On September 12, 2001, Dan found himself stuck in a Sofitel Hotel in Paris with little cash and no wallet. Fortunately, Diners Club called him back with a temporary replacement number that he would be able to use until he reconstituted the other lost portions of his wallet. For what was supposed to be a short trip, he planned to take a two-day holiday from the Internet and e-mail. But with all the uncertainty about how long he would be stuck in Paris, he decided to use the hotel's Ethernet and get online. After scanning through dozens of unimportant messages and spam, he opened the e-mail from Tom Kingsfield. After reading it over a dozen times, he wondered if he was still in the middle of a nightmare.

He looked at the results of his complete blood count one more time. *I'd be better off in a jet crashing into the Terminal Tower.* All of this, of course, explained his excessive fatigue for the past several months. *I missed it in Michael and I missed it again.* He had already taken on a mountain of stress and bad news in recent weeks: constant pressure from Weichel to travel less and increase clinical revenue, loss of his RO1, a pending jury trial for an alleged wrongful death, failure to land the coveted Pittsburgh position *(who cares, Kathy wasn't going to move there anyhow),* a stolen wallet while traveling alone in a foreign country, and oh yes, the whole world going crazy with jets flying into buildings.

But with this e-mail, the mountain turned into an erupting volcano.

Dan suddenly remembered Eze. He made a few quick calls about travel details, checked out of the hotel and was on his way. He thought about calling Kathy but decided against it. *She will think I'm crazy — maybe I AM crazy — this is all insane.* He felt tired but pleasantly content on the long train ride to southern France. *Damn, I wonder if they sell Glenlivet in Eze.*

He settled instead for drinking Chateauneuf-du-Pape, the wine originally created by monks during the Avignon Papacy — a seventy year period during which the popes were displaced temporarily from Rome to southern France. His initial plan was to drop off the face of the earth — the $8,000 limit on his Diners Club card would likely cover his life expectancy. *I could live here until I die.*

On his second day in Chateau Eza, he awoke in the late morning, surprisingly with no hangover. In fact, his mind was never clearer. He stood on his balcony, high above the Mediterranean Sea. The night before, he envisioned himself jumping into the sea. But now he felt at peace. Finally, that old glimpse of a mysterious reality had evolved into a new understanding. Much as Kathy had always taught her children, "God has a reason for everything," he now had a strong feeling that, some day, a collective consciousness would make all of this understandable, all serving a purpose. He recalled John Lennon saying, "If there is a God, it's all of us." Kathy and John Lennon were now both making sense.

The possibility of dealing with his own near-death experience brought it all into perspective. It was all about survival. Some people were surviving cancer, some were surviving ignorance; others were surviving violence and terrorism. Survival brought all human beings closer to a collective consciousness. Failure to survive set the whole race back a few steps. With each generation, the survivors advanced to the next step. Is this what Michael appreciated so quickly in the early days after his diagnosis? Dan might be able to walk away from his complicated professional life to deal with his new illness, but he was not capable of abandoning his wife and family. He was going to make every effort to survive.

It was too early back in Ohio to call Kathy. Hopefully she got his e-mail from the day before. Maybe she was on her way to France already. He would shower, maybe have some breakfast and then call his family in Solon to explain everything and find out whether Kathy was en route.

On stepping out of the shower to dry off, he looked down and saw that his legs and lower torso were covered with petechiae: tiny red-purple blotches resulting from bleeding capillaries in the skin. He wiped the steam off the bathroom mirror and saw a trickle of blood dripping from his nose. He suddenly felt faint, had a sudden urge to defecate, and collapsed to the floor.

He woke up hours later in a hospital in Nice with a very uncomfortable nasogastric tube in place in his left nostril. A young doctor — no older than twenty-five and presumably an intern or resident — spoke to him in broken English.

"Monsieur, you have had some serious internal bleeding."

"I'm a physician," Dan interrupted.

"Oh, yes, well, we have transfused four units of packed red cells thus far for severe gastrointestinal bleeding. You were quite hypotensive on admission, but your blood pressure has normalized with the blood and saline infusions. In fact, your blood pressure is now frankly elevated. Monsieur, please, may I inquire of any past medical history?"

"Long history of hypertension — usually take enalapril and hydrochlorothiazide — but not for several days — guess I just forgot. I just recently received the results of routine blood tests suggesting a blood disorder of some kind. I'm scheduled for tests back home. Can we please get this tube out of my nose?"

"Oh yes, well, we'll wait till my attending gives the word about your NG tube. *Even in France, the interns and residents apparently lived in constant fear of the wrath of their attending physicians.* You have severe thrombocytopenia and you will need platelet transfusions. Our consulting hematologist suspects that you have leukemia and would like to arrange transfer to Paris as soon as possible."

Dan sat up to protest — *Damnit I just arrived here from Paris!* His head was throbbing and he suddenly felt the lights going out once again.

Two days later, he awoke in the intensive care unit at Hopital Necker. He reached up to touch his own face. Good news — no nasogastric tube. This time, a senior physician, wearing a white lab coat that matched his thick white hair and beard was leaning over his bed.

"Bonjour, Dr Ulek. Are you with us?"

He recognized the physician to be none other than Henri Glotz, appearing a little older and perhaps more hirsute than he recalled from photographs in old journals.

"Where am I? What happened?"

Henri oriented Dan and explained that he had sustained a mild intracranial hemorrhage related to a very low platelet count and elevated blood pressure — now both under control after platelet transfusions and intravenous nitroprusside, a potent blood pressure-lowering agent. "Fortunately, the hemorrhage was a small one in the pontine area of the midbrain, so there are no focal neurologic deficits. The vascular accident only affected your consciousness."

Dan apparently was unresponsive for almost thirty-six hours during which he had a number of procedures including a CT scan of his head, and an upper GI endoscopy and a colonoscopy to look for a bleeding site in his gastrointestinal tract. *Kingsfield will be happy about the colonoscopy.* No bleeding site was found and the GI hemorrhage was thought to be related to diffuse oozing resulting from the low platelet count.

"We also performed a bone marrow biopsy. The bad news is that you have acute myelogenous leukemia. The good news is that we have performed genetic studies and you have an AML variant resulting from a translocation of chromosome twelve and fifteen."

Dan was embarrassed to admit that, despite Michael's illness, he had not kept up with the literature on the genetics of AML. "And that means?"

"Relatively speaking, the prognosis of this variant is excellent — better than most other forms of acute leukemia. Although chemotherapy will be needed, the remission rate is high and many long-term remissions and cures have been reported with chemotherapy alone in over 80 percent of patients."

Dan told Glotz the story of his son, Michael.

"Fascinating! It would very interesting to know Michael's genetic profile, but these studies were not being performed in 1994. I know Susan Sampson quite well. I'm sure she is busy now as Department Chair, but I will call her eventually. Perhaps we can obtain genetic studies on your son, but then it depends on whether his chromosomes now are his or those of your daughter. The science still mystifies me. We all are very curious about the possibility that some of these genetic variants of AML may be hereditary, or possibly related to common environmental exposures in genetically susceptible individuals."

Dan still had a headache, felt extremely weak, and had a sudden desire to skip the scientific lingo and slip into the role of a sick patient. But he was mesmerized by Henri Glotz' unique personality and his keen scientific mind.

Glotz went on, "By the way, it is a great honor to meet you, Dr. Ulek. I listened to your keynote address the other day and have always admired your work."

The compliment put Dan back into scientific mode. "Please, call me Dan, and the pleasure is all mine. I'm also aware of *your* work. I never thought we would achieve immune tolerance in our time, but your work has convinced me otherwise."

Side effects of immunosuppressive drugs were currently one of the downsides of organ transplantation. Immunologists like Glotz spent their careers looking for ways to fool the human immune system into failing to recognize an organ transplanted from another individual as foreign tissue. Fooling the immune system into recognizing the transplanted organ as "self" would allow transplantation without immunosuppressive drugs. Borrowing from the field of bone marrow transplantation, Glotz reasoned that a modified bone marrow transplant using marrow from the same individual who donated the solid organ might create chimerism — essentially a bone marrow with two immune systems content with two "selves." Glotz had proven that the technique was successful in monkeys and was ready to begin clinical trials in humans.

"And congratulations on your new position at Pittsburgh State," said Dan. "Tom Stallings told me the news at the symposium a few days ago. Moving from Paris to Pittsburgh should be an interesting change in cultures for you."

"Oh, indeed, I met with Dr. Stallings over coffee before the symposium was shut down. *Another cappuccino? Stallings must have been high on caffeine by mid-day!* It was a difficult choice, but I called him the next day to turn down the offer. It would likely take more than a year to dismantle our primate lab and reassemble it in Pittsburgh. Personally, I think I may be getting a little too old to take on the kind of administrative responsibilities that they were expecting from me. I really feel that I have several more years of productivity to offer as a scientist and physician. But more importantly, and as always, it boiled down to my wife's wishes. She loves it here in Paris and wasn't ready to go back to the United States. And honestly, the events of 9-11 didn't help with a decision to move to the United States right now."

A nurse walked in and asked Dr. Glotz if the patient could have a visitor.

It was Kathy.

Twenty-Nine

Ohio —
Late September –
Early October 2001

Based on Henri Glotz's prognosis, Dan agreed to treatment with chemotherapy. After a great deal of discussion about where the chemotherapy should be administered, he expressed his preference to return home for the treatment and was transferred to the Cleveland Medical Center after his condition stabilized in Paris.

It was unpleasant being a patient — much worse than the vicarious experience with Michael. Instead of a Broviac, he had a different contraption called a mediport. Its surgical insertion was less invasive than placement of a Broviac, but the mediport was used mostly for infusions and was less efficient for drawing blood — so like the patients he cared for during residency, his routine blood tests were often drawn from peripheral veins and he ultimately felt like a human pin cushion, covered with bruises. And what idiot ever decided that vital signs were needed in the middle of the night? Don't even begin to talk about hospital food. The chemotherapy was definitely unpleasant, but he developed his own liking for ondansatron and Demerol *(a whole family of junkies)*, although he somewhat favored good old fashioned morphine sulfate. He had nightmares about fungal infections, ventilators, leg amputations, and other surgical procedures, but thankfully, none of those awful complications ever materialized. As Henri Glotz predicted, an early remission was achieved.

While hospitalized, Dan had a long line of well-wishers and visitors. One of the first was Jack Hurtuk. Yes, the transplant service was surviving in his absence, but of course everyone was hoping that he would be back soon. No, Darlene May did not expire and was doing surprisingly well.

"I'm not sure if you are aware of what's going on with the Pittsburgh situation?" Hurtuk asked.

Dan had actually not thought much about his professional troubles during the past two weeks, but thinking about it now, he presumed that Jack had been offered the position after Glotz turned it down.

"Honestly, no."

"Well, it won't be *me* moving to Pittsburgh, that's as much as I know." Dan could tell that Jack was not willing to discuss the possibility that Dan was now the leading candidate. Given Glotz's turndown, Dan honestly didn't know what PSTI's strategy would be at this point.

Norma called from Dan's office. Yes, the office was managing in his absence, but everyone was hoping that he would return soon. No, he didn't need to worry about coverage. Weichel arranged for an urgent faculty meeting and adjusted the attending schedule for the remainder of the year, presuming that Dan would be out for a few months.

"Are you up for dealing with a growing pile of mail and messages?" she asked. "I'll walk them over to your room. Nothing urgent, except Dr. Tom Stallings has been calling from Pittsburgh almost twice a day for the past week. He knows your predicament, but says he needs to talk to you whenever you are up for it."

Is he calling to wish me well? Did they change their minds after Glotz turned them down? Would they consider offering a job of that magnitude to a man recently diagnosed with acute leukemia?

Bill Matthews stopped by to visit. "Great news, Dan, the Bennings case has been dropped."

"We settled out of court?"

"No, the case was dropped — permanently. In response to an expert witness' opinion, the patient's wife broke down and admitted that her husband had not taken any of his immunosuppressive drugs for several months prior to his terminal admission. When they did pill counts and checked with his pharmacy, it turns out he probably never took a single capsule of the so-called mistaken medication — so the allegation that his kidneys were damaged as a consequence of the wrong prescription didn't hold up."

"Doesn't explain why he presented with severe renal failure."

"Apparently, he had been taking large doses of ibuprofen for back pain. I talked to John Jacobs from Renal and he thought that it was a plausible cause of the kidney damage. Anyhow, we're off the hook. Now get well soon. Everybody wants you to back to work as soon as possible."

As he went through his mail from the past three weeks, he came across a letter from Redicon Publishing. He had only submitted his latest book in early August and wasn't expecting a response so quickly. The envelope was thin. He recalled that, when applying to colleges years ago, thick envelopes were good, thin envelopes a sure sign of rejection. Not so today. Based on their internal reviews, the folks at Redicon were anticipating a series of bestsellers — and were hoping to sell up to a half-million copies of each book. Dan read and re-read the offer for royalties on sales of his first three books, and the proposed advance for additional novels. He did some quick arithmetic in his head, trying to recall how British pounds converted to U.S. dollars. *Holy shit.*

Of course, one of Dan's most important and regular visitors was his son, Michael. Strangely, when Michael visited, there was very little conversation. Instead, he would bring a CD player from home, along with some CDs of rock and roll songs that his Dad had played for him in 1994 and 1998. Clearly, Michael remembered each and every song. Dan even recognized songs that he had played for Michael when he was intubated and presumably comatose. Only now did he understand that Michael heard them all. Each song brought back vivid memories — some good and some very bad. There was no need to talk. Long ago, Dan realized that Michael had come to an understanding of the collective soul at a very young age. As they listened one night to Beck singing "Where It's At," Dan looked at his son and had a new appreciation of hope and survival.

Dan was discharged home in late November. He needed some home physical therapy and was instructed to take at least a month off from work, save for light-duty paperwork at home. He found himself thinking less about medicine and more about his next book. *Maybe one with a happy ending.*

More than ever, it was great to be home. As he crawled into his own bed for the first time in weeks, he thought about how wonderful it was to be in bed with his wife. He was still too weak to even think about sex. He just wanted Kathy's companionship and the wonderful sensation of cuddling under the covers on a cool autumn night.

He figured it was time to tell Kathy that Tom Stallings called and offered him the Pittsburgh job last week. They were not concerned about his leukemia as they had checked with the CMC oncology team who felt that his prognosis was excellent. Stallings realized that, under the circumstances, Dan would need time to recover and talk things over with the family before making a decision.

"Dan, I want you to know that I have been tormented by the Pittsburgh thing since 9-11," Kathy said. "It was so wrong for me to object to a move. I realize now that I was being selfish. I am so proud of you. I am your wife and I will follow you anywhere."

He leaned over and kissed Kathy on the lips.

"If you won the lottery, would you quit your day job?" he asked.

Wow, that came out of the blue. "What are you talking about?"

He reached into the drawer of the nightstand next to the bed and handed Kathy the letter from Redicon.

"Oh, my god, Dan. I thought your book was great, but I didn't know you were thinking of publishing it. This is fantastic. Ummm, Dan — What's a British pound worth in dollars these days?"

"I'll have to check. You know, Kath, a friend of mine recently reminded me that life is short. I know my medical prognosis is relatively good. And I hope that Michael's is even better. But I'll live the rest of my life concerned about each of us relapsing. I've thought about this a great deal, and I don't think I can deal with concerns about RO1s, RVUs and lawsuits at the same time."

After a pause, he went on. "I called Stallings yesterday and turned down the job."

"I also called Rick Weichel and told him I was taking an *extended* leave of absence."

"Remember those beautiful villas in St. Tropez? As soon as I'm strong enough, I'm going back there to buy one. Will you follow me?"

Dan closed his eyes. Kathy looked at him and wondered what he was thinking. *Maybe he's saying a prayer.*

Thirty

Newark Airport — September 10, 2001

Dan sat at the gate, staring at his laptop. He couldn't concentrate on the powerpoint slides that he had put together for tomorrow's talk — actually it was a reassembly of slides that he had used many times before. Instead, he found himself reflecting on his behavior during the past several months. He certainly hadn't been much of a father to his children or a husband to his wife. Although he had been taking care of sick inpatients for three consecutive months, he had become preoccupied with Paris and Pittsburgh and increasingly was disenchanted with his day job. Thank goodness for Deb Hepner. The patients were always in good hands with Deb running the ship — even when her master clinician had his head in the clouds.

He looked down at his feet and realized that he was wearing a black sock on his left foot and a brown sock on the right. *Who cares? No one will notice.*

For some odd reason, Dan's thoughts drifted to a conversation he had with his father many years ago when he was home for the summer after his junior year in college. It was one of the few "man-to-man" talks that he ever had with his father. Dan had just applied to medical school. His father always questioned his decision to study medicine — even after he started medical school. He thought a business degree would be more profitable and secure: "maybe someday be an executive for a utility company — we're always gonna need utilities." Dan found this to be interesting advice from a man who never went to college, grew up in a coal-mining family in West Virginia, and migrated to Ohio to find factory work.

Whenever Dan was asked, "How did you decide to become a doctor?" he spouted off the usual stuff: wanting to help others, stamping out disease, etc. Looking back, Dan realized now that he was motivated less by altruism than by a burning desire, not just to have a better life than his parents, but to make a *quantum leap* in stature and success. He might have achieved the same stature as a lawyer or maybe even as an executive in a utility company.

Although Ed was perplexed about Dan's career choice, he was proud of his son's accomplishments and ultimately acquiesced. "Whatever it is that you decide to do, be true to your heart. Do the best you can — always try to be the best at what you do." Although Dan felt that he was never very close to his father, this one piece of advice resurfaced from the back of his brain on virtually a daily basis.

I am trying to do my best. Am I being true to my heart?

A crying infant in the waiting area jolted Dan's mind out of the daydream. He didn't even hear the boarding call for business-class customers. *Here I am questioning my career choices just as I am off to the most important meeting of my life.* He had an overwhelming sense that his life was about to change dramatically after this trip to France. *But will the change be good or bad?*

He clicked off Powerpoint, but before powering down to board the plane, he switched to Word, pulling up the file containing the latest novel he had secretly submitted to Redicon earlier in the summer. Suddenly, the story seemed all wrong. He wondered if it was too late to recall the manuscript and revise the final chapters.

Thirty-One

Pittsburgh, Pennsylvania —
February 2005

Dan was more nervous than usual about being a visiting professor and giving a talk. He had been through the routine a hundred times. But this was going to be his first invited talk in more than four years, and he would be speaking to some notable physicians and scientists at the Pittsburgh State Transplant Institute. He couldn't resist the invitation from his former colleague, Jack Hurtuk, who asked him down for a two-day visiting professorship. He would give an hour-long talk at Transplant Grand Rounds, and also spend two days meeting with various faculty members and trainees to discuss clinical programs or research projects. And of course, he would enjoy a small group dinner with the PSTI leaders at one of Jack's favorite Mt. Washington restaurants. Jack also asked Dan to bring Kathy for an extra day, so that the Hurtuks and Uleks could have a nice dinner on their own, rekindling their old Valentine's Day tradition.

In early 2002, Jack was recruited to the PSTI, not as the program director to replace Tom Stallings, but as the institute's first president. He was now 62 years old and most of his work was administrative in nature, including a lot of schmoozing with philanthropists. He saw patients only rarely and scrubbed in the operating room only at the request of fellow surgeons when they were in trouble with difficult cases. He had little time to be involved directly with research projects, but he served as a consultant to review and critique research protocols, and also edited most manuscripts prior to their submission for publication — so that he was a prominent co-author on fifteen to twenty publications each year. The PSTI was possibly the busiest transplant center in the world and certainly the most academically prolific. Jack fit in well as the institute's president.

Dan and Kathy drove from Solon to Pittsburgh — less than a two-hour trip. They turned down the Hurtuk's offer to stay at their home on the Ohio River in Sewickley, and instead stayed at a hotel in downtown Pittsburgh. The plan for the first day was for Dan and Kathy to pick up Nancy in Sewickley in the late morning, to check into the hotel, and then to drop the wives off for lunch in the city while Dan headed for the University for the first half-day of his visiting professorship. Dan was amazed at Nancy's appearance. Since he last saw her in 2001, she had lost at least 20 pounds, was wearing her hair longer and a bit lighter, and actually was wearing lipstick and a touch of makeup. She looked ten years younger.

"Nancy you look terrific. Looks like life in Pittsburgh has been good to you," said Dan.

"I was so reluctant to make the move, but we both love it here. It was best thing that ever happened to Jack. He loves his job and seems more relaxed than he was at the CMC. It's amazing to have my husband home almost every weekend."

"You look so fit and trim. I'm jealous," said Kathy.

"I followed your lead and started a walking program a few years ago and also go to an exercise class two or three times a week. I also stopped drinking about three years ago. Have never felt better. So the bad news is — I won't be drinking wine tonight at dinner. The good news is that there will be more wine for Jack and Dan and I can be the designated driver!"

As Dan left Kathy and Nancy to head to the PSTI, he said "I can hardly wait for dinner tonight — will be fun to catch up on the kids."

After meetings with three research scientists, Dan had an hour to meet with Jack before giving his Grand Rounds talk. They hadn't seen or talked to each other for more than three years. Like Nancy, Jack looked great and it was immediately obvious that he was less stressed than he was as the surgical director years ago at the CMC.

"Well Jack, here I am — I finally made it to Pittsburgh!" Dan joked.

"You are most welcome, Mr. Famous Novelist. Hey, I've read all of your books — I love them all, except for the parts about me. Was I really that much of a prick back in Cleveland?"

"Why, Jack, those books were not about you," Dan lied. "So tell me what this president thing is all about. They must have changed the job description after the summer of 2001."

"Yes, I think that Stallings and the other leaders here reconvened after Glotz and you both turned down the job and decided to restructure the organization. I preside administratively over six program directors. My clinical responsibilities are minimal and you know what? — That's been okay with me. I spend a lot of time flying all over the country — and the world — asking rich people and corporations for money to support the institute. Since I took the job, our endowment has doubled in size."

"Dr. Jack Hurtuk, *traveling* around the world?" Dan asked in amazement.

"Yep, and I bring Nancy on many of the trips — she loves it."

"Quite a departure from your lifestyle in Cleveland. I thought you hated to travel and also hated when I traveled."

"Dan, you never realized how I envied your lifestyle when we worked together in Cleveland. You were traveling and becoming internationally famous. Don't get me wrong, you deserved every bit of it. But as a surgeon, I honestly felt intensely guilty about leaving my patients to be covered by colleagues. When I opened someone's chest to bypass their coronary arteries or to replace their sick heart with a new one, I felt an absolute responsibility to follow the patient until they were completely healed."

"I always appreciated that, Jack — but are you happy that you walked away from patient care?"

"Yes, I am very happy. Transplantation is a field for young surgeons. I remember the early days when I would be awake for more than thirty-six hours — first flying somewhere to harvest an organ, then flying back to do the transplant, and then going back to the operating room to deal with some urgent complication. I'm too old for that kind of physical stress. But more importantly, it was the mental stress that I needed to walk away from. It was affecting my interactions with colleagues — I really *was* a prick — but it also was interfering with my marriage and my family life. Life is short, you know?"

Do I ever. Dan realized that, after knowing Jack for more than twenty-five years, he was having a meaningful conversation with him for the first time. He suddenly felt like he was talking to a *friend*, not just a *colleague*.

"So, Dan, what the hell happened to you? Word was that you fell off the face of the earth — famous medical novelist living a secretive life on the French Riviera. Then all of a sudden, I hear you're back working at CMC. Talk about a departure in lifestyles. What changed your mind about being a Renaissance man living in the South of France?"

"What changed my mind?"

He went on, "It was Michael. Jack, it was my son, Michael."

In September 2003, Michael sent an e-mail to his father after he returned from his summer vacation in St. Tropez. At that

point in time, Dan and Kathy were debating about officially re-
tiring, selling their home in Solon, and making St. Tropez their
permanent home. Tom was already living in Columbus and the
other three kids were in college, leaving the Solon home literally
empty. The e-mail from Michael changed all of their plans. Dan
printed the e-mail and kept it handy, often re-reading it:

Dad:

Good to be back in school. You know, Bowling Green
is almost as pretty as southern France at this time of year
— LOL. I can't speak for Lauren or Brian, but I had a
great time this summer at your new villa in France.
But I don't think it's your home. You and Mom
looked so happy and relaxed in St. Tropez. I think it's terrific that you've taken up writing and painting. I'm sure
you're making more money writing books than you were
making as a doctor. But Dad, it's not your home. I am not
talking about a physical place. I'm talking about a spiri-
tual home — what you do, why you are on the planet.
Do you remember writing in your books about 'catching
a glimpse of some new consciousness' or something like
that? I think you know that I had the opportunity to catch
that same glimpse as a young boy, and I have never let it
go. As your son, I'm telling you that it's time for you to
come home.

Love,
Michael

Dan told Jack the story about their summer in St. Tropez
and about Michael's e-mail. He felt that he was sharing some
intimate secrets with a true friend.
Dan went on, "Have you ever read Thomas Wolfe's novel,
You Can't Go Home Again? Well, I think someday I'll write a
book called *You Can Never Leave Home*. My son taught me that

I was deceiving myself by taking on a new life in a new place. Like Michael, I had survived a life-threatening disease. But my son was a true survivor. I used the illness as an excuse to leave my real home. That wasn't survival — it was an escape. Kathy had made a decision to follow me anywhere, but I realized that I had displaced my wife from her real home as well. I've had chances to escape to St. Tropez and to Pittsburgh, but Michael set me straight. I've been back at CMC since late 2003. I'm busy as ever, but my attitude is different. I care for patients differently. I really *care* for them. Kathy and I used profits from my novels to establish a research foundation that now funds my own research and the research programs of six other physician-scientists in the division. And Jack, save for this drive down the turnpike to see you and Nancy, I *never* travel to meetings or talks. We now only travel for *real* vacations. I finally feel like a survivor, and I feel like I'm at home. "

There was a long pause in the conversation as Dan and Jack looked at each other, recognizing that this was the beginning of a new kind of friendship.

Jack looked at his watch. "It's almost four o'clock and time for your Grand Rounds talk. Let's head down to the auditorium and get your slides loaded. I don't even know today's topic — are you going to talk about tacrolimus, immune monitoring assays, or maybe some new research project?"

"None of the above. Actually, I didn't bring any slides. I'm just going to tell a story. I am going to tell Pittsburgh a story about survival."

Thirty-Two

2011

Jack Hurtuk retired in 2009 and moved with Nancy to an oceanfront home on Cape Cod. Their children, Steven and Susan, are both married and remain settled in California, each with two children. Jack and Nancy travel to the west coast frequently to see their children and grandchildren.

Michael is working in Chicago as a case manager in a nursing home for disabled children and is still hoping to apply to nursing school. Tom married his high school sweetheart and lives in Columbus. He was a late bloomer. After bartending for a year after graduating from Ohio State, he returned to school to get his MBA and now works in the marketing department of Key Bank. Lauren moved to L.A. after graduating from Notre Dame and is attending film school while working part-time as an assistant director. Brian earned his PhD in molecular biology at George Washington University and works for a biotech firm in Washington, D.C.

The kids are all grown and gone, but more than ever, they are at home. Dan and Kathy are enjoying their empty nest. They sold their villa in St. Tropez and bought a smaller, less expensive second home in Sanibel, where they vacation twice a year. Dan has become fond of the change in seasons in Ohio. He also listens to Motown music now and then. He cancelled his publishing contract but still writes novels — when he is in the mood.

The Ulek kids return to Solon every year for the week before Christmas to exchange gifts, to catch up on each others' lives, to recall Black Monday — and to celebrate another year of survival.

Epilogue

Parents should die before their children. Nothing is sadder than the death of a child, but a near-death experience can be just as taxing, often changing the lives of parents and other family members. The story about Michael is 90 percent true. The remainder of the story behind *Racing to Pittsburgh* is 50 percent untrue, but is based on some serious realities.